ANN EVANS

Ann Evans spends all her time writing. She is an award-winning feature-writer on the *Coventry Evening Telegraph*, as well as the successful author of several children's novels. Ann penned her first book in her spare bedroom after seeing how much her children loved reading horror stories, and since then she has gained a considerable reputation for fast-paced psychological thrillers.

She was inspired to write *The Beast* after holidaying in Scotland and noticing how the light over the lochs can play tricks on your eyes…

The Beast

USBORNE THRILLERS

Terry Deary
The Boy Who Haunted Himself

Sandra Glover
Demon's Rock

Malcolm Rose
The Tortured Wood

Paul Stewart
The Curse of Magoria

Tim Wynne-Jones
The Boy in the Burning House

The Beast

ANN EVANS

USBORNE

For Wayne and Mel
with love

First published in 2004 by Usborne Publishing Ltd., Usborne House,
83-85 Saffron Hill, London EC1N 8RT, England. www.usborne.com

Copyright © Ann Evans, 2004
The right of Ann Evans to be identified as the author of this work has been
asserted by her in accordance with the Copyright, Designs and Patents Act,
1988.

A CIP catalogue record for this book is available from the British Library.

ISBN 0 7460 6034 3 Printed in Great Britain.

Chapter One

Karbel's yellow eyes sparkled as a shaft of sunlight glanced off the rock. The immense beast didn't blink or squint. The sunlight no longer dazzled and blinded as it had when he was of this mortal world. Now nothing of this earth troubled him.

He could see great distances. Travel as fast as the wind. Visible only as a fleeting shadow that might catch someone's eye and make them puzzle for a moment as to what they'd seen – or thought they'd seen.

Now, as in countless years gone by, Karbel lay, stretched across the smooth granite ridge, high on the Scottish mountainside overlooking his domain.

From here, as ever, he watched the forest as it changed in colour and shape, as seasons came and went. Seeing it now, rich and lush green under the summer sun. Later it would slowly curl into autumn's gold and then winter's freezing wind and snow would strip its branches bare before the new buds reappeared in spring, completing the eternal cycle.

Lazily, Karbel's yellow eyes moved to scan the loch. Deep and cold with its surface of glass and its icy hue, where he once swam and fished. Where once, long, long ago, he splashed and played as a cub, where he would cool off in summer, where he hunted. It was in that loch that he could, in one swift, precise movement, skilfully scoop a fish from the water on his long, razor-sharp claws.

Now there was no need for him to cool down in the heat of summer. Or find warmth when snow fell. Now he had neither hunger nor thirst to satisfy. The spirit world had no mortal needs.

Yet sometimes Karbel was overcome with the urge to feel and taste – and *kill* again. He was a hunter. He was born with the instinct to kill.

That instinct, like his soul, was eternal.

Sometimes, the need became too overwhelming, and he would summon up every drop of energy within his spirit to grant himself a brief spell of mortality. Too brief, but sufficient to satisfy his cravings for a time.

Karbel savoured these moments that left his spirit almost wiped out. But it was worth it to feel again, briefly, the warm earth beneath his paws, the taste of crystal-clear stream water, to enjoy the thrill of the hunt and finally the tearing and devouring of fish or flesh.

Stretched out now on his ridge, overlooking his valley, something caught his eye.

Far, far below, on the outskirts of his forest there was movement.

Humans!

As he watched, a low almost silent growl purred from his jaws and he slunk lower onto his belly, the instinct always there. That too, like his spirit, had not died.

Humans often came to his valley. Usually when the sun was at its hottest. They would stay a while, making their noises, flattening the grass and burning the wood from the forest. Then they would leave and the valley, with its silence and beauty, would once again be his.

Karbel had no love for humans. Indeed, it was because of a human that his life had been cut off in its prime so many winters ago.

At the memory, Karbel threw back his head and a high-pitched howl echoed out across the valley.

To anyone listening it would have sounded like the howl of the wind, but still a hawk launched itself swiftly off the rock face and flew high into the cloudless sky.

Karbel's attention returned to the humans and something stirred within him. There was something familiar about one of them – the young male.

Karbel recoiled, his lips drawing back from his fangs, spitting and hissing as he recognized the boy.

Yet it could not be. The boy who had put an end to Karbel's mortal life would have grown old and died by now. It had been so many years.

Centuries.

But the young human down in the valley had the same look. The same build, the same fiery red hair – even from here Karbel could sense that same fearless spirit.

It *was* him!

Karbel's yellow eyes became slits of hatred.

He had returned – somehow.

How?

Perhaps humans had the power to be reborn.

But why had he returned?

Instantly Karbel knew the answer. There could only be one reason. Many centuries ago, the boy had taken Karbel's mortal life. Now he had returned to take his spirit.

"No!" Karbel howled out. He would not allow that to happen.

In a flash, Karbel recalled that fateful day. His final day. A day which could never be erased from his memory.

It had been a long, bitter winter, millennia ago. Snow was up to his belly and he was hungry. In the valley there had been a human settlement which normally Karbel kept well away from, but that winter hunger forced him to venture near. It would be easy pickings to snatch a human's baby offspring.

Hunger drove him into the settlement. Under cover of a dying winter sun that blinded the humans to his presence, he slunk on his belly, picking up on the scent of human flesh, slavering at the jaws. He sought his prey, small and easy to snatch and escape with, to devour at his leisure in the safety of the mountains.

He recalled the adrenaline coursing through his veins as he had crept closer to his prey. A female baby human, wrapped in blankets and lying in a cot just inside a tent. Karbel had moved silently, yet somehow the infant sensed his presence and began to scream. A terrified, high-pitched cry that alerted the other humans.

Karbel knew he had to move quickly. He sprang towards his helpless prey, but from nowhere rushed a boy. A boy with flaming red hair and piercing grey eyes. A boy with no fear – and a dagger in his hand.

Jumping in front of the baby human as Karbel sprang, the boy thrust the dagger clean into the beast's heart.

Karbel's spirit was ejected violently from his mortal body and he witnessed his own lifeless, bleeding carcass drop into the snow.

The face of the boy without fear was etched into his soul. And now, as Karbel looked down into the valley he saw that same face. Recognized that same fearless spirit.

But this time the boy would not win the battle.

This time he, Karbel, would be victorious.

This time Karbel would kill first.

His spirit flared within him. The power and strength were still there to be called upon. He stretched out his massive paws and his razor-sharp claws unfurled, slicing clean through the rock, yet leaving no imprint.

He curled his black lips and two long, white, deadly fangs glinted in the sunlight. Throwing back his mighty head, he roared a silent, fearsome roar towards the heavens. Nearby a bird took flight, screeching and protesting against the unknown, unsettling movement in the wind.

Then, barely noticeable, a tiny pebble fell from the ridge. Dislodged by an invisible presence, it rolled and bounced all the way to the valley floor.

Chapter Two

Down in the valley, on the edge of the forest, twelve-year-old Amanda Laird shivered.

She rubbed her arms, surprised to find them covered in goose bumps. Above stretched a cloudless blue sky. The sun was at its hottest, already colouring her arms honey-brown.

Yet she shivered.

Close by, her parents were making sure the caravan was level, and her elder brother, Grant, was lugging the blue frame tent from the boot of the car.

It wasn't just her skin that was cold. She was shivering inside too, the sort of shiver that made her skin prickle and the hairs on the back of her neck stand up.

She looked around. It was a beautiful valley. Named Endrith Valley after a battle between two clans who fought each other to the death hundreds of years ago – or so their mum had cheerfully informed them as they'd driven here. "Known locally as the Valley of Shadows," she had quoted from the folklore book she'd bought when they stopped earlier.

Amanda gazed across the peaceful valley. It was hard to think that this had once been a scene of horror and pain. Perhaps that was why she felt so jittery. Perhaps she was picking up vibes from this ancient battleground.

She took a deep breath of pine-scented air. She had been looking forward to this holiday for so long…but now that they were here, she felt odd…

"Hey, Manda!" Grant yelled as he struggled with the bag of tent poles. "Do you intend standing there like a dummy all day, or are you going to give me a hand?"

She shook herself, trying to throw off the odd, foreboding sensation that had coiled around her like a damp, cold mist. "I'm coming!"

"About time. Here, you drag the tent poles. I'll take the tent."

He headed off towards the forest, the canvas

bag balanced on one shoulder. He was big for fourteen – most people thought he was older. Big and strong and good looking – according to all her friends at school. They all thought she was so lucky having a brother like him.

She supposed she was, really. As brothers went, he was okay. Annoying, but okay. And why was he lugging the tent so far away from the caravan. "Grant! Where are you going to pitch it?"

"Over by the forest," he called over his shoulder.

Amanda glanced back to her parents' caravan. She could feel an unreasonable panic rising inside her. "But we'd be safer staying nearer the caravan with Mum and Dad…" Her words died away. *Safer?* What was she talking about?

Why on earth did she suddenly feel that they were in danger? She shivered again, her grey eyes darting this way and that, searching for something…something she couldn't even put a name to.

"What are you scared of? Big bad bunny rabbits?" Grant called, sticking out his front teeth and hopping about like a demented rabbit.

"Hey what's up Doc, got any carrots?"

Amanda laughed. She was being silly. There was nothing to be afraid of. It was probably just the unfamiliar landscape.

"Come on, Manda, hurry up with those poles."

"I'm coming!"

She dragged the bag of poles through lush green grass that was dotted with tiny white flowers. To her right was a massive forest of pine and silver birch trees. Directly ahead stretched a mirror-smooth loch, and to the left were the beginnings of the mountain range.

The natural beauty was breathtaking. Perhaps it was the immense open space that had unnerved her. The total lack of any kind of civilization. The echoing isolation.

She breathed deeply. The air was so clean. She ought to be relaxed, not on edge and constantly looking over her shoulder.

Grant was way ahead, intent on camping as far away from their parents as possible. She called out again. "Grant, that's far enough, isn't it?"

He stopped and looked around. "I suppose."

She caught him up, dropped the bag of poles onto the grass and gazed around. With the sunlight filtering through the branches on the edge of the forest, it looked a fascinating, inviting place to explore. She tried not to imagine what it would be like in the dead of night.

"We're a long way from Mum and Dad," she remarked, trying to sound casual. The caravan seemed miles away. Would their parents hear their cries for help?

She shivered again. What had put that thought in her head? She had absolutely no intention of crying for help. What was there to be afraid of? They were in Scotland, not the jungle.

Grant pulled the tent from the bag and spread it over the grass.

"The further the better. You know how Mum fusses. Now then, I reckon we should pitch up close to the forest edge. That way the trees will give us some protection."

"Protection from what?" Amanda demanded, alarm resounding in her voice.

Grant frowned at her. "What's up with you? I only meant protection from the wind and the elements. What did you think I meant? Monsters and ghoulies?"

"Well, I don't know," she said dismissively, feeling stupid. "There could be anything living in the forest. Foxes, wolves…"

"Foxes won't come near you. They're scared of people."

"What about wolves?"

He shrugged and pushed his flame-coloured hair back from his eyes. Grant had the same slate-grey eyes as Amanda. The same wild red hair. No one could doubt they were brother and sister. He stood pondering the question for a moment. "Mmm, I suppose it's vaguely possible that there could be a wild wolf on the prowl. I read that in some parts of Scotland wolves are being introduced back into their natural habitat. But even if there are wolves, they wouldn't come anywhere near us. They'd stay well away from civilization."

"We're nowhere near civilization," Amanda remarked, knowing her unease wasn't based on being frightened of a wolf. It was nothing so logical.

No, this was an ominous feeling, as if something was heading towards them. Something she couldn't see. Just something…

Something bad.

They pitched their two-man frame tent, with a little help from their dad, at the edge of the forest. The blue nylon tent was big enough to stand up in, with two inner sleeping areas. Each compartment zipped to keep out creepy crawlies. Mum came over with squash and sandwiches and they all sat outside on a rug, eating, drinking and making plans for the week.

"Isn't this glorious…" sighed their mum, gazing out over the loch. "I'm going to paint this scene so we remember it for ever."

"Have we been here before, Mum?" Grant

asked as he helped himself to another sandwich.

"No, we should have come though. It's so beautiful."

"So we didn't come here when I was little?"

Amanda frowned at her brother. "Why?"

Their mum smiled. "No, first time for all of us. Pass me the squash, would you?"

Amanda remained curious. "Grant, why did you think we'd been here before?"

He shrugged. "Don't know. It just feels a bit familiar. *Déjà vu*, you know."

Dad finished off the last sandwich. "*Déjà vu* or not, I think we'd all better take a walk. See what's here. That way we'll be able to lay down the ground rules for you two. We don't want you wandering too far away or straying anywhere dangerous."

"Okay," Grant agreed, jumping to his feet, eager to explore. "Come on, then. What are we waiting for?"

They set off, walking around the edge of the forest, then heading down towards the loch. Grant took off his trainers and rolled up the bottoms of his jeans.

"Watch out for Nessy." Amanda grinned, feeling more relaxed now they were together in a family group. *Safety in numbers*, a little voice in her head said.

"Wrong loch, dummy," Grant replied. Then, suddenly, he yelled and began hopping on one foot. "Help! Something's got me!"

Amanda's blood turned cold. Grabbing Grant's arm, she dragged him so quickly and fiercely from the water that she almost sent him flying across the grass. Her own strength surprised even herself.

"Steady on!" Grant gasped, staggering. "Crikey, what did you have for breakfast?"

"I thought something was biting you!" she snapped, feeling stupid for overreacting when he was only messing about.

Her brother grinned. "I didn't know you cared."

"Idiot!" Amanda retaliated, giving him a thump.

Mum raised her eyebrows. "I hope you two aren't going to bicker all week."

"Manda's worried in case there are wolves on the loose," Grant explained, paddling in the water again.

"I doubt that very much, love," said her dad. "The rarest creatures you'll find around here are the pine martens, and they're only little things."

"They've got sharp teeth, though," Grant teased, pretending to nibble the ends of her hair with his fingers.

Amanda shrugged him off. "I know what a pine marten is; it's a sort of weasel with a bushy tail."

"And there are bound to be deer and otters," added their mum, as she delved into her shoulder bag. "Actually, you'll be able to tell us what wildlife there is. I bought these nature books earlier. You'll be able to identify butterflies and animal tracks and things." She brandished two booklets.

"I'll have mine later," Grant said, bending to examine something in the water.

Amanda took hers, managing to smile and wishing she wasn't so jumpy. "Thanks, Mum. This will be really interesting."

"They might keep you pair occupied so your dad and I can enjoy a relaxing week," she added, linking his arm.

"Hey, look!" said Grant, scooping something from the water. He held his cupped hands towards Amanda as their parents strolled on. "It's teeming with tiny minnows."

Amanda half expected him to throw the water into her face, but he managed to refrain and when she looked she saw the tiny fishes for herself. "Oh, wow! The loch must be swarming with little fish."

"Big ones too, I hope," their dad called back.

Amanda started to feel happier, and she gazed around at the magnificent landscape as they wandered on. She had never imagined Scotland would be so beautiful. It really was incredible, with its dramatic mountains and the huge expanse of greens and greys and blues.

As they neared the lower parts of the mountain range, the ground became rockier. And here they discovered that the loch was fed by trickling mountain streams that cascaded between boulders and over ridges.

From a distance, the nearest mountain had looked impressive. Close to, it was awesome. It began as a gradual ascent, from a patchwork quilt of moss and bracken and boulders at its base, rising up to a majestic rock face that towered above them, its bleached granite walls pitted with deep crevices and precarious ledges.

"I could climb that," Grant murmured.

"Yes, I can just see Mum letting you!" Amanda remarked, as she shielded her eyes from a shaft of sunlight glinting off the rock. "She'd have a fit— Oh! What's that?"

"What?" Grant asked, looking up.

Amanda squinted as she peered upwards to where something had caught her eye. But there was nothing. Whatever she'd glimpsed had vanished now. She frowned. "I thought I saw something."

"Could have been a hawk," Grant suggested, walking on.

"No, it wasn't a bird," she replied vaguely, still

looking up. "It was just...something."

Frustrated at not being able to put a definite shape to whatever had caught her eye, she continued staring up at the ridge, expecting whatever it was to reappear.

But there was nothing there. Nothing at all.

"That's odd," she murmured, rubbing her arms as goose bumps broke out all over them. "I must have imagined it."

Grant glanced back at her. "Well, this place is nicknamed Valley of Shadows, isn't it?"

"Yes."

"Probably just a shadow, then."

His suggestion did nothing to erase the chill that crawled over her skin. She'd always been afraid of shadows.

Chapter Three

They had barbecued steaks for their evening meal
with salad and tinned potatoes. With a gas-powered
refrigerator in the caravan, there were few home
comforts they did without.

"With any luck we'll have trout for tomorrow's
tea, once I get my rods out," Dad said cheerfully.
"Grant, fancy a spot of fishing tomorrow?"

"So long as I can chuck back whatever I catch,"
he said, pulling a face.

Dad laughed. "You'd be no good as a hunter."

"Too right!" Grant agreed. "You won't catch me
killing anything, not even a fish."

"I didn't see you turning your nose up at that

steak," his mum remarked lightly.

"That's different. It was just a piece of meat. I didn't have to see it alive and running about first."

She smiled. "I know. I'd be just the same if I had to hunt for my dinner. I'd end up living on berries."

"Me too," Amanda agreed. "And Dad, if we *must* eat fish tomorrow I don't want to see the heads!"

Everyone shuddered in agreement, except Dad. "What a bunch of wimps!" He laughed.

Darkness fell. They sat around the caravan watching a magnificent red sun sink into the distant horizon of the loch. The blood-red water swallowed it up, leaving behind only a fading orange glow in the sky.

Mum had set up her easel and was painting madly, trying to capture the blaze of colours in the sky before they faded. "I can't do it justice. I've never seen such a brilliant sunset."

"Nor me, it's really beautiful," murmured Amanda, putting on a sweatshirt as a cool breeze fluttered across the valley.

"Well, I'm going to make a campfire over by our tent," Grant announced, stretching himself, then gathering up a few stones and twigs. "Come on, Manda. I'll show you how to make a fire by rubbing two stones together."

She looked doubtfully at him. "Mmm, and when

that doesn't work, we'll ask Mum for a box of matches."

Grant humoured her with a half-hearted smile. "Have faith will you. I've got skill...I've got badges!"

"Are you sure you want to camp out?" their mum asked, glancing up from her painting, a tiny frown etched across her forehead.

Amanda hesitated. Being tucked up safe and sound in the caravan, with her parents close by, seemed the best option, only that would mean Grant sleeping on his own. Not that he was worried. But wasn't that half the problem? She was the one feeling uneasy, not him. If Grant felt anxious, then he'd be on his guard...watching...listening.

On his guard against what? she asked herself.

She had no answer.

"No, we'll be fine, Mum," she replied, trying to convince herself more than anyone. And with a confident smile she ran after Grant, picking up sticks as she went.

Over by their tent, he arranged some stones into a little fireplace and made a wigwam of little twigs and bits of paper. Then he sat, cross-legged, rubbing two pieces of flint together in an effort to create a spark.

Amanda dutifully sat and watched. After ten minutes, she suggested she fetch the matches.

"No way... Look! I got a spark then. Did you see it?"

"No."

"Well, I did."

Growing bored, she got up and wandered a little way along the edge of the forest. They were on holiday for a week – she couldn't spend all that time being afraid to venture more than a few steps away from everyone. Deliberately facing up to her fear, she walked a little way into the forest, shining her torch up into tree branches and along the forest floor in the hope of catching a glimpse of some wildlife. To her delight, she spotted a rabbit. For a moment it sat, staring mesmerized into the torch light. Then, with a hop, it disappeared into the undergrowth.

"Grant! I've just seen a rabbit," she called.

"Got big buck teeth, had it?" Grant called vaguely, still engrossed in his fire-making.

"Ha ha!" she muttered, following the beam of light from her torch deeper into the forest, hoping to catch sight of another woodland creature. There were probably deer – one could be watching her right now. She shone her torch left and right, stepping over tree roots and disentangling herself from bracken. Oddly enough she felt quite comfortable surrounded by the trees. It was almost as if they were protective – shielding and guarding her. No, the forest was not a place to be afraid of. This wasn't where her unease lay. She felt good here, deep within the friendly forest.

Her confidence growing, Amanda wandered deeper still, her torch beam leading the way as she investigated the chirping of insects, holes in the bark of fallen trees and strange-looking fungi. Then, suddenly, her torch failed.

Darkness engulfed her.

A total, black, overwhelming, suffocating darkness.

She let out a little gasp of surprise and clicked the torch switch back and forth. It refused to work and she banged the torch against her hand. Still nothing.

Without sight, her hearing became acute. The sounds of the forest were more intense. She could hear the sound of fluttering leaves and the creaking and groaning of branches. Why were they groaning? It was almost as if they were stretching...stretching out to catch hold of her. After all, it wasn't just dead wood – it had never been *dead* wood. Now she felt the lifeblood of the forest. Now she sensed its living, breathing presence. She could almost hear its breath fanning against her face, so slow, so deep, yet breathing nonetheless.

Wide-eyed, and her heart thudding much too

fast, Amanda tried to get her torch working as the fluttering of leaves began to sound like whisperings. As if the trees were softly murmuring to each other – talking about her. A stranger in their midst. Friend or foe…

She shivered. That same hair-prickling shiver as before. Was she a fool to have trusted the forest? Had it lured her inside with a false sense of security, only to trap her and…

And what?

She tried to stay calm, speaking out loud to herself. "Okay, so the torch has died, so what? Mum and Dad are just over there…"

She turned and headed back the way she had come, but the rough bark of a tree barred her way.

Wrong way! You're going the wrong way! A voice in her head screamed.

Determined not to panic, she let her eyes grow accustomed to the darkness. Looking up, the sky at least was lighter. A distant moon brightened the outline of grey scuttling clouds, as if edging them with a silvery pencil.

Only at ground level was the darkness overpowering. Menacing. Tree trunks took on human form. A whole army of tall, straight wooden beings that might uproot at any second and trample her into the ground. Or close ranks and crush her to death.

"Grant! My torch won't work!" she called out, feeling her panic rising.

No reply.

"Grant!" she yelled louder, edging past the tree, only to find her way blocked even more. The undergrowth was becoming denser, the ground more mossy underfoot.

"I'm going the wrong way," she breathed, annoyed at her own stupidity. *Stay calm.* Panicking was not going to help.

She took a steadying breath and peered all around, trying to figure out which way to go. She hadn't walked far, she couldn't be *that* lost. So long as she remained calm she would find her way out.

"Grant! Hey, Grant, I'm not sure which way to go."

Silence greeted her.

Raising her voice, she shouted as loud as she could. "Grant, can you hear me? Mum! Dad! Hello…!"

Something scampered from underfoot and shot away. Amanda started to tremble. Her throat felt dry. She turned this way and that, disorientated in the darkness.

Quite suddenly, she saw a light glinting far off through distant trees – but it was too far away to be the light from Grant's campfire or their caravan.

She froze. What was it?

Was it Grant, searching for her? Could she possibly have walked that far, and in totally the wrong direction?

Or was it something else?

"Grant!" she called. "Grant, is that you?"

She stared hard through the blackness. What was it? Someone else's torch light? Or the eyes of some woodland creature watching her? It looked like lights from a window, but could there really be a house so deep into the forest?

Another caravan, maybe?

She began to feel hot and cold in turns. Cold sweats, hot panics. She turned frantically, straining her eyes through the darkness, looking this way and that, trying to spot a familiar landmark.

Then, suddenly, she glimpsed other lights – two blocks of light, not far away but half obliterated by the trees. With a great sigh of relief she realized it was their caravan.

Stumbling over roots and bracken, she scrambled her way back to the edge of the forest. Finally, breathlessly, she emerged into the clearing and stared at the deserted, unlit campfire. Her heart lurched.

"Grant! Grant, where are you?" she cried out, feeling sick inside. "Gra—"

"Keep your hair on! I'm coming."

Amanda spun round to see her brother walking back from the caravan with a box of matches. Her knees felt weak with relief, but with the relief came anger. "Didn't you hear me shouting for you?" she demanded, aware that her heart was thudding wildly against her ribcage.

"No, I was searching for the matches." He looked mildly defeated, unaware of her brush with fear. "Why are you staring at me like that? You were the one moaning about not being able to light the fire."

"I was shouting for ages," she continued, annoyed with him for not being there when she needed him. "My torch stopped working and I couldn't find my way out of the forest."

Grant took her torch and fiddled with the batteries. Flicking the switch, a bright yellow beam shone into her face.

She felt useless. "Oh. Why wouldn't it do that for me?"

"Skill." He shrugged. "If only I could get this stupid fire to light as easily."

"Yes, well, perhaps the twigs are damp," Amanda murmured as the thudding of her heart returned to its normal rhythm and she began to relax.

She spotted her parents then, arm in arm down

by the loch. She turned her attention to her brother. Kneeling down by his campfire, cupping his hand around a match. She smiled to herself. She was stupid to have panicked like that. There was nothing to be afraid of here. This was a beautiful, peaceful, tranquil place.

Nothing to be scared of here at all.

Chapter Four

Later, as flames from the open campfire danced and flickered in the darkness, they all sat around its warmth toasting marshmallows.

Popping a final one into her mouth, Mum yawned. "Time for my bed I think. Kids, are you sure you wouldn't rather sleep in the caravan? It wouldn't take long to make the beds up."

"Not for me," Grant said adamantly.

"Nor me," said Amanda, determined not to get nervous again. "It'll be lovely and cosy in the tent."

"Well, if you're sure..." Their mum sighed, getting to her feet.

Dad followed. "Let the fire die down now and

make sure you zip your inner tent up or you'll be overrun with creepy crawlies during the night."

"We will. Goodnight," said Amanda, yawning.

Air beds cushioned them from the hard ground as Amanda and her brother crawled into the inner tent a little later.

"It's lovely and cosy, isn't it?" she called through the thin flap of linen dividing the two sleeping areas, as she snuggled down into her sleeping bag.

"Yeah, warm too."

"Dark when you turn the torches off, though."

"Not scared are you?"

"No!" Amanda answered truthfully.

"Sure?"

"Positive!"

"G'night then, Manda. Don't snore too loudly."

"I don't snore," she responded, settling down and letting her eyes become accustomed to the blackness. For some time, she lay awake, listening to the sounds of the night, and thinking. It had been a strange day. Feeling uneasy, but not knowing why, she plumped up her pillow and made a decision. She wasn't going to let it bother her any more. Endrith Valley was a fantastic place to camp and she was going to enjoy every minute.

Eventually, she drifted off to sleep, only to wake up suddenly some time later, not knowing why. But her eyes sprang open and her heart was thudding.

For a second, she struggled to work out where she was. Then the silkiness of her sleeping bag reminded her. It was still pitch-black, no dawn light penetrating the tent yet. Close by, the steady sound of her brother's breathing told her he was still fast asleep.

Her heart continued to bang away, alarmed at waking so suddenly. She strained her ears listening…trying to catch the sound that had woken her so abruptly. Perhaps an animal was scratching about outside. Or maybe she had just been dreaming.

She dragged the sleeping bag over her ears, determined to get back to sleep. Then she heard something. A movement close by the tent. *Very* close.

The crushing of the grass. Almost silent – but not quite.

She held her breath, her eyes like saucers in the darkness.

"Grant!" she hissed. "Grant – wake up."

He muttered in his sleep and turned over.

Amanda lay motionless. Too afraid to make any sudden noise or movement in case it startled whoever or whatever it was outside into doing something rash – like attacking them.

Instead she lay rigid, her breathing shallow, her ears acutely tuned to every sound. There was definitely *something* outside. Human, animal, she couldn't tell. But she sensed it there – just at the other side of the thin fabric of the tent.

It could be her dad, checking on them. Yet, somehow, she doubted it was him. She began to tremble.

Lying there, clutching her sleeping bag, her wide eyes followed the movement outside. It was circling the tent, as if curious – or looking for the way in...

"Grant, wake up," Amanda hissed. But her brother slept on, oblivious to the danger.

She fumbled for her torch, intending to use it as a weapon if necessary. As her fingers gripped the handle, she sensed something else. She sensed the creature, whatever it was, moving away. There was no distinct sound, there were no footsteps telling her it had lost interest. She simply knew it, and the prickling sensation at the nape of her neck faded away.

When she was positive it had gone, she scrambled out of her sleeping bag and the inner tent, then scuttled across the groundsheet to unzip the outer flaps enough to peer out.

Brilliant silvery moonlight illuminated the landscape, transforming the mountains and forest outlines into picturesque silhouettes. The loch shimmered like a gigantic looking-glass. For a second, the beauty blinded her to everything else. Then a movement caught her eye. A movement at the edge of the forest. Something, or someone, vanishing amongst the trees.

Amanda caught her breath. It was a woman! She was almost positive that she glimpsed a skirt flapping around her legs. But she couldn't be sure and she rubbed her eyes, annoyed for not spotting the figure sooner. Now it had gone, and all she was left with was a niggling feeling that history was repeating itself. *Déjà vu.* This was the second time she'd felt as if she'd just missed catching sight of something.

She frowned, trying to recall the first time. But her brain was still fuddled with sleep. With a sigh, she zipped up the tent and crawled back to bed.

Her imagination was playing tricks on her.

"Sleep well?" Their mum greeted them as the smell of sizzling bacon lured Amanda and Grant towards the caravan the next morning.

"Like a log," said Grant, buttering a piece of toast.

"How about you, Manda?"

"Oh, yes. Fine," Amanda said cheerfully, deciding not to say anything about the previous night. There was no point in worrying her parents over nothing. It was just her stupid imagination anyway.

"So who's coming fishing with me today?" Dad enquired as they tucked into their breakfasts.

"Not me, I'm for sunbathing and painting," Mum replied, glancing out of the caravan door at another clear, sunny day.

"Grant?"

"No, thanks, Dad. Manda and I are going exploring."

Amanda raised her eyebrows. "Are we?"

"Yep."

She glanced at her mum and shrugged. "We're going exploring."

"Don't wander too far away, now," their mum said. "Remember what we agreed yesterday."

"No probs," Grant agreed.

"And you could take those nature books. That should keep you busy."

Amanda glanced through her book as she ate. It was packed full of information about wildlife and flowers – and included a fascinating section on animal tracks. After breakfast, she took it back to the tent and examined the surrounding grass for evidence.

"What are you looking for?" Grant asked, intrigued.

"Footprints." She glanced up at him. "There was something snooping around our tent last night."

"Was there? I didn't hear anything."

"I know you didn't!" Amanda said accusingly. "I tried to wake you."

"Did you see what it was?" her brother asked, looking mildly interested.

The memory of the skirted figure disappearing into the forest sprang back into her mind. "The only thing I saw looked like a woman going into the forest."

"Could have been Mum."

"Going *into* the forest – in the middle of the night?" Amanda stressed, raising her eyebrows.

"Another holiday-maker then."

"Possibly. Actually, I think there *is* someone else with a caravan parked in the forest. I saw a light through the trees last night."

"You didn't say."

Amanda shrugged, getting to her feet, disappointed at not finding any footprints. "Nothing much to say. I just saw what looked like light from a house or caravan through the trees. Anyway, where are we going exploring?"

"I quite fancy a closer look at those mountains. It looks brilliant over there."

"Well, as long as I don't have to climb anything. You know what I'm like with heights."

"It's a deal."

Walking around the edge of the loch, they eventually reached the lower slopes of rocky ground. Here the earth was swathed in tough green moss and grey shale, with rocks and boulders, tiny streams and shallow caverns.

Amanda shielded her eyes from the sun to look up at the crevices and ridges high above. If there were wolves, wouldn't this be the ideal place for them to sit and watch? She flicked through her nature book for paw prints.

There was nothing about wolves.

They spent an hour or so exploring and Amanda identified a dozen different types of flowers and ferns shown in her book. When they came across the cave, it took them both by surprise.

"Oh, wow! Look at this, Manda. A real prehistoric cave."

"Don't go in!" Amanda reacted instantly, her voice sharp. The shadowy black hole was the most intimidating thing she had ever set eyes on.

The opening was about head-height and wide enough for two people to go through together. But inside it was pitch-black and even the air surrounding it felt icy cold.

"Wonder how far it goes in?" Grant said, taking no notice of Amanda as he peered inside. "Crikey, it's cold in here." His voice came out as an echo as he ventured deeper into the darkness.

"Come out, Grant," Amanda called, rubbing at the goose bumps on her arms. "It might not be safe."

"Nah! This has been here for centuries. I bet there are cave drawings on these walls. Wish I'd got my torch."

Amanda waited uneasily at the entrance to the cave, straining her eyes to keep track of Grant's white T-shirt moving around in the blackness. Her skin prickled uncomfortably. "Grant, I really wish you'd come out. You might get lost or there could be snakes or anything."

"It's okay," he called, his voice sounding as if it were coming from a long, deep tunnel. "I'm feeling my way carefully. It goes well back. We'll have to come back with torches Manda – this is brilliant."

"Okay, we will," she called, indulging him. Anything to get him out of there. "Only come out now before it caves in or you fall down a pothole."

"Okay, I'm coming."

She held her breath, half expecting to hear his cries for help at any second. When he finally emerged, she breathed a huge sigh of relief.

Grant looked exhilarated. "That was brilliant! You'll have to come in with me, Mand."

"I don't like caves. They're spooky, especially

that one. I don't know how you dare go in."

"It was great – it goes ever such a long way back."

"Wonderful. Now, come on, let's see what else is around." She was anxious to be away from the horrible black hole as quickly as possible. It gave her the shudders.

Grant was reluctant to leave but Amanda turned her back on him and walked on, picking her way over fallen boulders, knowing he would follow eventually. He caught her up just as something in the distance caught her eye.

"There's someone over there," she said, as he scrambled over the massive chunks of granite that littered the mountain. She stared down into the valley at the figure heading their way.

Grant climbed up onto a big rock and sat, dangling his legs over the edge. Then he grinned. "Look at this guy! He's wearing a kilt."

Amanda cast her brother a withering glance. "Hello? We *are* in Scotland, remember. It's where kilts come from."

Watching the elderly chap as he strode nearer, Amanda was quite impressed with his outfit – a kilt, sporran, tartan socks, a beret, and a nobbly old walking stick, which he swung as he walked, as if keeping time with a military band.

As he got closer, Amanda saw that the unruly mass of greying hair that stuck out from beneath his tartan beret had once been a rich auburn.

He waved his stick cheerily. "Halloo! It's a grand day to be out walking."

"Yes, it's lovely," Amanda replied, edging a little closer to her brother, remembering her parents' constant warnings about talking to strangers.

The elderly Scotsman pushed his stick through his leather belt as if stowing a sword into a scabbard and smiled, his face crinkling like a piece of corrugated cardboard. Then he gazed all around. To the left, then right, upwards at the mountain above them, then turning to glance back the way he had come.

Finally, he focused directly on Grant and Amanda, spearing them both with steely, grey eyes – a searing glance that made Amanda feel as if he could tell what they were thinking. Then in a dialect that was as Scottish as he looked, the man said, "You'll be the bairns camping out in the valley, I'll be bound."

"Yes, that's us. How did you know? Did you see our tent and caravan?" Amanda asked, suddenly wondering whether he could have been the skirted figure she had glimpsed last night.

"Aye, that I did, lass," he said, his steely eyes

missing nothing. "I've lived here in the Valley of Shadows all my life. I like to keep abreast of who's visiting."

Amanda glanced at her brother, wondering if he was thinking the same as her. Actually, she hoped this old man *was* the figure she'd spotted disappearing into the trees. If so, he wasn't half as scary in reality as the horrors her imagination was tempted to conjure up. She held out her hand politely. "I'm Amanda Laird and this is my brother Grant. Why do they call it the Valley of Shadows?"

They shook hands. He had a cold hand despite the warmth of the day. Cold but with a remarkably firm grip. "Just legend," he dismissed, snatching his beret from his head and bowing flamboyantly. "The name's Rab Stewart. At your service. How long will you be staying?"

"Just the week," Amanda told him, amused by his old-fashioned manners.

"A week," he repeated, his eyes squinting as if he were trying to work something out. Then he nodded, saying flatly, "A whole week. Why, that's grand."

Amanda stared at him. He didn't sound like he thought it was grand. He sounded like he thought it was a headache. Perhaps he was possessive about his valley. Perhaps holiday-makers weren't welcome at all.

"Where do you live, Mr. Stewart?" Grant asked, leaping down from the rock and towering over the old Scotsman.

For a second, the old man seemed taken aback by Grant's size. He looked at him in the way an aunt would stare at a child she hadn't seen for a long while, and say, *My! Hasn't he grown!*

Amanda couldn't take her eyes off them. Then the moment passed and the old man said, "Me? I have a wee cottage in the forest."

"There, I knew it!" Amanda exclaimed, this latest bit of news taking her mind off her puzzled thoughts. "I saw a light through the trees yesterday evening."

"Did you now?" Rab Stewart nodded, seeming almost to lose interest in them for a second. Far more interesting, suddenly, was the sheer rock face above them. He looked up, squinting his eyes as he scanned the ridges, as if searching for something.

Amanda was fascinated by his eyes. They were so pale, almost transparent. Sharp, alert, watchful eyes. Not old, yet eyes that had seen everything there was to see. Ageless eyes.

Seeming satisfied that there was nothing above to concern them, his old face crinkled as he focused his attention back on them. "Do your parents know where you are?"

"Oh, yeah." Grant nodded. "We've had our orders."

The old man nodded. "Well, make sure you don't wander too far, now."

"Why?" Amanda asked curiously.

"In case you get lost, of course," he answered, glancing back now across the valley, his eyes never still for a moment.

"Do you work here, Mr. Stewart?" asked Grant. "I mean, like a forest ranger?"

"Aye, sort of. Every now and then I get called out of my retirement, so to speak. When I'm needed to keep an eye on things."

"And are you keeping an eye on things now?" Amanda asked cautiously.

He fixed her with an intense gaze, making her shiver as he said simply, "Aye."

"Keeping an eye on us holiday-makers," Grant suggested suspiciously. "Making sure we don't fish the loch dry or burn the woods down."

The man's face crinkled. "Och! Nothing like that. Holiday-makers are as welcome as the flowers in May. No, it's just my job to make sure you come to no harm."

The shivery sensation rushed down Amanda's spine. "Harm? Harm from what?" she asked softly.

"Why, nothing specific," the old man answered

quickly. Too quickly, Amanda thought. "But I've lived here all my life. I know the place like the back of my hand. So, should visitors get lost, I can usually find them before they have to call out the mountain rescue."

Amanda wondered if that was the truth, or whether he was hiding something.

With a deep breath, the old man turned back towards the valley. "Well, I'll leave you bairns in peace, but I'll pop by and say hello to your parents later. No doubt when you tell them you've been gossiping to a stranger they'll be anxious to know all about me."

"They'd love to meet you," Amanda said, honestly. Even if he wasn't telling them the whole truth, he meant them no harm. She was positive of that.

He drew his stick from his belt, reminding Amanda of some highland warrior of long ago, drawing his sword before going into battle. She couldn't help but smile. Perhaps that was how he saw himself. Protector of the innocent. Guarding them all from wild bunny rabbits and elusive pine martens.

Waving them a cheery goodbye, he strode off, picking his way across the rocky terrain. Amanda glanced at her brother, who was grinning from ear to ear. "Nice, wasn't he?"

"Nutty as a fruit cake, if you ask me," Grant replied.

"Well…yes, probably. But he's still nice."

Grant gazed after the kilted old man as he headed towards the forest. "How about we check him out? Let's go and find his cottage in the forest."

"Why?" Amanda frowned. "It's not very nice to spy on him."

"No? Well he was spying on us last night, wasn't he? All that nonsense about making sure people don't get lost. We weren't reported missing, were we? So why check on us? It's a bit dodgy if you ask me."

"Well…I suppose," Amanda reluctantly agreed. "Anyway, he won't know we're checking out his cottage, will he? We could just say we were exploring the forest when we came across his house. I mean, we won't be going in or anything."

"No, of course not," Grant said, picking his way down between the rocks. "So what are we waiting for? Come on."

Chapter Five

From the murky blackness of the cave, Karbel's yellow eyes peered out towards the archway of sunlight. Slowly he rose up from the undisturbed dust at the furthest point within the cave, where he had lain undetected. He stretched his mighty spirit body and padded towards the cave opening. His paws were silent, making no impression in the dirt of the cave floor.

Karbel snarled a low, guttural growl as he emerged into the sunlight. The boy had come looking for him. But he had been too clever and had merged with the shadows, lain still while the boy came closer, unaware of his ghostly presence.

Not even when the boy had been standing almost on top of him had he sensed Karbel's presence. Nor when Karbel had lashed out with his massive paw and his claws had cut straight through the boy, had he felt anything. He had remained intact and blissfully unaware of what should have been instant death.

Angry and frustrated, Karbel had lashed out again and again, spitting and snarling. In his mortal lifetime, nothing could have withstood such an attack, but now his rage could not even disturb the dust particles that hung in the air. And those razor-sharp claws that sliced through the boy were as fatal as a spring breeze.

Now Karbel padded outside the cave entrance and stood, looking over the valley. The days were young. It took time for him to manifest himself into mortal form again. Time and immense willpower were his tools. He had to summon up every ounce of strength and desire, and focus it on his one desperate need to become mortal again, just briefly.

But long enough.

And now that mortality was gathering. He could feel it. Beginning deep within his spirit body he sensed a throbbing beat, a pulse, as his heart once more pumped blood through his veins.

Soon he would be mortal again. His need was great. Summoning up all his willpower, he would achieve his goal. But he had to focus. To centre all his hatred on the boy. The boy who had taken his life so many millennia ago.

Revenge would be his. A few days was all he needed. Until then, he would watch and wait and stalk his prey. And slowly he would become powerful again. And then the boy – this boy with flaming red hair and a fearless spirit – would be sorry.

He began to slaver at the mouth as mortal desires took hold. The urge for flesh and blood always accompanied his brief spells of mortality.

This was his time for preparing. For concentrating on those desires and needs. His rage was growing, and with rage came strength.

He sprang, stretching his lithe body as he leaped and pounced from rock to rock, as light as the air, until he could see the boy and the girl in the distance, walking towards the forest.

Watching them, he crouched down on a rock, and found the scent of the young human male still lingering there. In anger, he scratched at the rock surface, and this time saw the faint outline of claw marks left on the stone. Thin, white marks, barely visible at all.

But there, just the same.

He settled down, yellow eyes fixed upon his prey in the distance, and purred to himself.

Soon...

"Well, I can't see any cottage," Grant complained, as they snaked their way through the forest. "I reckon our Mr. Rabby Stewart was fibbing. Are you sure you saw a light somewhere around here?"

"Positive," Amanda said as she trailed behind her brother. In daylight, the forest was a beautiful, fascinating place to explore and she had jotted masses of findings down in her nature book, from fungi and trees to berries and woodland creatures. Grant hadn't even glanced at his book.

In places, the forest opened up into large grassy clearings, where fallen trees lay smothered in moss and ivy, their stark branches jutting out at weird angles, making them look like dead aliens. In these clearings, the grass had grown waist high and shafts of sunlight streaked down between the sparse trees, warming the earth, making everything glint and sparkle.

"Try and remember which way you were facing when you spotted the light," said Grant, stopping to look all around.

Amanda sighed. "It's difficult to tell. I'd lost my bearings – I hadn't a clue which way I was going."

"Well, we've walked round in circles for ages. If there was a cottage here, we'd have found it by now." He sat down on a pile of ivy-smothered stones

54

and rubble and took a carton of orange from his backpack. "I reckon we should ask him exactly where his cottage is, if he turns up at the caravan. Not that I think he will. I reckon he's just the local nutter."

"I quite liked him," Amanda disagreed. "There was something sort of reassuring about him."

Grant's eyebrows shot up. "Reassuring? He was a right weirdo. And I don't fancy the idea of him wandering around our tent in the middle of the night."

Amanda shrugged. "Oh, well. We probably won't see him again. Let's head home, I'm starving."

"May as well," Grant said, gulping down his drink. Getting up, his foot skidded on some damp moss. "Whoops! Watch you don't slip over, Manda. There's a slate or something under all this moss." He scuffed his foot over the ground, dislodging the weeds to reveal some flat grey stones. "Hey, I wonder what these were?"

Amanda stepped over the stones, being careful not to slip. "No idea. Come on, let's get back. I think we've done enough exploring for one day."

"Okay, I'm definitely ready for some lunch. Hey, Manda. It's this way."

With a hopeless shrug, Amanda turned and followed him, glad his sense of direction wasn't as bad as hers. They emerged from the trees near their tent. A little way off they spotted their parents sitting around the caravan. They weren't alone.

"He's there!" Amanda gasped, grabbing her brother's arm.

"Who? Crikey, it's him!" Grant exclaimed.

Rab Stewart spotted them and waved.

"Hello again!" Amanda called, breaking into a run. Reaching the caravan, she flopped down onto the sun lounger next to her mum's.

"So you're back at last," said Mum, pouring two more glasses of squash. "Mr. Stewart says he met you by the mountains. You weren't climbing, I hope, Grant?"

"Nah, just messing about on the slopes. Found a wicked cave. We're going back with torches to see if there are any cave drawings on the walls."

"Don't be daft, Grant—" Amanda began, but Rab Stewart held up a hand.

"You'd be surprised," he said knowingly. "There's definite evidence that primitive man lived in these parts as far back as the Iron Age. Ancient beasts lived here too."

"Mr. Stewart knows all about this valley," Dad added, topping up the elderly Scotsman's glass with more orange squash. "Kids, help yourselves to sandwiches. Mr. Stewart, another ham and pickle, or some more pork pie?"

"Aye! That would be grand," he said, tucking in like he hadn't eaten for a week.

"Where exactly do you live, Mr. Stewart?" Grant asked, glancing at his dad. "He was telling us he had a cottage in the forest."

"How lovely!" Mum exclaimed.

"Aye, it's a grand little place. Just tiny, mind. There's only me and I don't take up a lot of room."

"You live in *this* part of the forest?" Grant pressed, nodding towards the trees beyond their tent.

"Aye."

"But—" Grant began. Amanda immediately interrupted.

"It must be wonderful living in a forest," she said pleasantly. "But doesn't it ever get lonely? And what about buying food? We're such a long way from a town. Do you have a car?"

He chuckled at the very idea. "A car? Me? Heavens, no! What would I do with a car?"

Amanda glanced at her mum as the old man continued to chuckle to himself like it was the funniest thing he'd heard in a long while.

"I don't know how *we* would manage," her mum remarked. "But I imagine this is a much nicer, slower way of life. In the city, we always seem to be rushing around everywhere."

"Aye, I've a peaceful existence. My legs take me

everywhere I need to go." His face crinkled. "They may be old and knobbly, but they still work."

Amanda giggled.

Rab Stewart stayed until the last sandwich was eaten and the second jug of squash downed. He got to his feet slightly creakily.

"I'll take my leave of you, but if you need any help or anything just give me a call."

"What's your number?" asked Mum, reaching for a pen.

The elderly Scot chuckled. "A telephone! Och, no! I meant that you should just give me a call, shout my name. I'll hear you – sounds echo around the valley." He looked directly at Amanda. "You'll see."

She frowned, wondering if she'd imagined that he'd singled her out with those words. She tried not to dwell on it and joined the others to wave goodbye as he set off towards the forest, striding along with his stick swinging in time with the silent military band.

"What a sweet man," Mum declared, gathering the plates and glasses to wash up.

Amanda spotted her brother and dad exchange glances and grin at each other. She said nothing.

They all went for a long walk in the afternoon, way past the first big mountain to where the grassy, flower-strewn ground dipped right down into a fantastic green hollow. They took a football, which their dad and Grant hogged. But, as the hot afternoon sun blazed mercilessly down, it wasn't long before Dad gave up battling for the ball and left Grant to dribble it along as they explored the beautiful valley.

They were all hungry again by the time they decided to head back to camp. Grant led the way, mainly because he was hungriest, followed by their parents, who seemed to be taking endless photographs of the amazing panorama all around them.

Amanda dawdled way behind everyone, identifying lots of the wild flowers from her nature book.

She only realized how far behind she was, when she reached the brow of the hill that led down into their part of the valley. Way below, the caravan looked like a little dinky toy, and the tent a tiny triangle of blue. Grant was already at the edge of the loch, looking like a little dot, her parents not far behind him.

Her mum turned and waved up to her, then walked on, arm in arm with her dad. Amanda stood for a moment, enjoying the early evening breeze in her face, taking in the view. The sky was turning pink as the sun began to set, the few puffy white clouds seemed etched in gold. It was all so beautiful and so peaceful. It was hard to imagine how these flower-strewn hillsides must once have been bathed in blood, as highland tribes had battled to the death.

To her left, the awesome mountains reared majestically upwards, and she gazed up to their craggy ledges and beyond, wondering if the bird that was circling high above could be an eagle.

But then something else caught her eye.

A fleeting movement high on a ridge.

Like before, she thought instantly, as an icy shiver darted through her. She swallowed hard, finding that her throat had suddenly become parched. She wished now that the others weren't so far away. They weren't even looking this way.

Quickly, trying not to panic, she pushed her nature book into her bag, not stopping to pick up the pencil that slipped from her fumbling fingers. Then she quickened her pace determinedly and hurried down the long, sweeping slope towards camp.

Safety in numbers, a voice in her head whispered.

And she was all alone.

Chapter Six

The massive wall of rock to her left dazzled as the glaring sunlight glinted off it. Amanda hurried on, walking a few steps, running a few. From the corner of her eye, she sensed something watching from the mountain. She turned and squinted up. And saw it.

Or rather, she saw a movement. Nothing more than a shaft of light, as if cast by a cloud passing over the sun. Not solid. Not tangible. *There* but not there.

Valley of Shadows. Was this why it was so called?

The fear that gripped her was real enough though, and she started to run, wishing with all her heart that she hadn't dawdled so far behind everyone.

Running faster now, spurred on by the forces of gravity as she fled down the slope, she managed to snatch swift glances at the mountainside. The streak of light was still there. She saw it shooting down the rock face. But it didn't move like a beam of light, in a clear straight line; it zigzagged from ridge to ridge, rock to rock, as if reflected constantly by mirrors. First one way, then another. But its progress was constant – moving downwards, closer and closer.

Her heart was thudding, pounding against her ribcage. Now she flew at top speed. Somewhere behind her, her hair bobble fell out and her long red hair streamed out like a brilliant flame. She didn't stop, couldn't stop.

From the corner of her eye, she saw the light hit the ground at the base of the mountain, then leap from boulder to boulder until it reached the loch.

Stopping for breath, Amanda pushed hair back from her face with her arm. She stared across the vast, smooth loch. Its surface was flat, with barely a ripple. She gasped and doubled up to relieve the stitch in her side. Again, she stared at the loch, where the flash of light had stopped. There was nothing. A trick of the light, that was all it had been.

But then her heart missed a beat and shivers ran down her spine again. There was a definite movement in the water. She shielded her eyes against the sparkling sunlight that danced over the surface. Something was causing a wake. Something invisible to her eye – or maybe it was just below the surface. But it was moving swiftly, leaving a V-shape of ripples on an otherwise mirror-smooth surface.

Something was out there, swimming. Swimming towards their camp.

"Dad!" she screamed at the top of her voice, as she broke into a frantic, desperate run.

He heard and turned around. "Look!" she cried, pointing out to the loch, as she pounded nearer and nearer. Her family turned to look.

"Can't you see?" she gasped, racing down onto the flat land of the valley. "Something's in the water…"

Her feet barely touched the ground. Her breath was snatched in desperate gasps, as she frantically tried to catch up with her parents before that *thing* reached the shore.

Her dad turned to face her. He was smiling. He didn't realize the approaching danger. He thought she was running like the wind for fun. He held out his arms.

Amanda tore on, her lungs screaming for air. It was there – at the water's edge. She saw the V of ripples heading right into the shallows.

"Woah!" her dad laughed, as she collapsed exhausted into his arms. "My, that was quite some run. Anyone would think you were in training for the Olympics."

She struggled free and spun round. "Watch out, it's here! It's here!" The V-shape wake dissipated as it reached the shoreline. "Grant?" she screamed, spinning this way and that. "Where's Grant?"

"Hey, steady on, love," her dad frowned, holding on to her arms. "What's the matter?"

"I saw something in the water!" Amanda cried frantically. "Something big, swimming this way. Look! Look at the loch! Look at those ripples!"

Her mum hurried over and put her arms around her. "Amanda, love. It's okay. There's nothing there. You probably saw a log drifting along. That's how Loch Ness Monster stories come about."

"No, I saw it come down the mountain and jump into the loch," Amanda gasped, still frantically looking round. "Where's Grant? Find him Dad!"

"I'm here," Grant said suddenly, peering out of the caravan door with a drink in his hand. "Hey, what's the matter with Manda?"

"Too much sun, I think," Mum said, walking her towards the caravan.

"I'm not imagining it, Mum," Amanda gasped, trying to look back as she was led into the caravan.

"It's the light around these parts. It can produce a sort of mirage," said her mum, pouring a glass of water. "And we've been out all day in the sun. Drink some water, love. You'll feel better in a moment."

"Close the door," Amanda gasped, expecting something to spring into their caravan at any second. "Get Dad to come inside and close the door."

Anxiously, her mum stroked Amanda's hair from her hot, damp forehead. "It's okay, there's nothing to be afraid of. And if old Nessie *is* out in the lake, she can hardly touch us on dry land, can she?"

"I'm not joking!" Amanda cried, jumping to her feet. "There's something out there. It can swim and it can climb. It came down from the mountain like a streak of light. It came straight for us. Dad, you've got to come in – now!"

At last, and as if humouring Amanda, her dad came into the caravan and closed the door after him. "Okay, pet. Don't panic, it's okay. Get that water down you, then I think we could all do with a nice cup of tea."

"Not for me," Grant shrugged, heading for the caravan door. "I'm just going—"

"No!" Amanda screamed at the top of her voice. "No, he can't go out there. It'll get him! Mum, *tell* him!"

Her mum's eyes darkened. In a whisper she said, "It's definitely the sun. She's got a touch of sunstroke. Just stay inside for a while, Grant. Humour her, she'll be all right once she's calmed down."

"Mum, I'm not suffering from sunstroke or anything," Amanda pleaded, tears in her eyes now. "You've got to believe me. There's something out there. Something bad."

Amanda's mum made her sit down, soaked a flannel under the cold tap and put it on her forehead. "Well, when you've cooled down we'll take a good look, okay? I mean, darling, we'll have to do something. We can't just stay cooped up in the caravan, can we?"

We could go home, Amanda almost said. But she couldn't get the words out. Her parents and Grant had been so looking forward to this holiday. She closed her eyes. Her head was throbbing. Perhaps it *was* too much sun after all. The pounding of blood in her brain made her sleepy. She closed her eyes.

She must have slept. She awoke to find herself lying on her parents' bed in the caravan. The door was open and voices drifted in from just outside. It was dark except for the light from their oil burners and the glow of red-hot charcoal on the barbecue. Sausages and beefburgers were sizzling on a griddle –

their smell drifted in, making Amanda's stomach rumble.

Her parents were drinking wine, while Grant was whittling a piece of wood with a penknife. They all looked up as she stood shakily in the open doorway.

"Hi," her mum said, smiling. "Feeling better?"

They were all okay. Monster or no monster, they hadn't been hurt while she slept. It must have been sunstroke after all.

"I'm thirsty," she murmured.

Grant poured a long drink of cold orange squash and handed it to her. "Here you go. Hey, you were really weird."

She said nothing, but sat down on a sun lounger and sipped her drink.

Grant continued staring at her. "In fact, you were pretty whacko before you passed out."

"Grant!" Dad warned.

He grinned. "Well, she was."

"I thought I saw something," Amanda said softly, feeling stupid now.

"Yes, and so have many other people," said her mum kindly. "That little folklore book mentions lots of reports of strange sightings in this valley. I'm sure it's the sunlight reflecting off the loch."

"Could be heat haze coming off the ground, too," said their dad, putting his arm around Amanda.

"Hungry, love?"

She nodded. "Mum, can I borrow that book?"

"Yes, of course. It's a bit dark to read, though."

"I'll read by torchlight when I go to bed."

They sat out until midnight. No one was in a hurry to go to bed. Eventually, however, even Grant started yawning.

"Well, I'm for my bed. See you in the morning, everyone."

"I'll go too," Amanda said, getting up and stretching.

Her mum looked anxious. "I think I'd be happier if you slept in the caravan tonight, love. The sun hit you really badly this afternoon."

"But I'm fine now," Amanda promised, watching Grant heading for their tent, disappearing into the darkness. "I'll be fine camping out, honestly."

"Well, if you're sure."

"I'm positive," she said, picking up the folklore book. "Goodnight... Grant, hang on! Wait for me."

"Come on, then," he called back, his vague silhouetted outline waiting in the blackness.

She gave her parents a quick goodnight kiss then walked towards her brother...walked, determined not to give in to any panic and run. But in the pitch-black abyss between leaving the safety of the campfire and her parents, and catching up with

Grant, she felt her skin prickle.

But nothing leaped from the shadows. She reached Grant and they walked over to the tent together. Grant flicked on their torches. "If they'd trust us with an oil lamp, it would be really cool."

"These torches are okay," Amanda said, shining her torch into every corner of the tent.

"Phew, it's like an oven in here," Grant said, peeling off his sweatshirt.

"Mmm," Amanda agreed, glancing at her brother. "Grant, I know you think I'm crazy, but this afternoon the feeling of danger was so real. It was like some invisible evil was coming at us… Oh! What have you done to your arm?"

"Where?"

She touched the top of her brother's arm. There was a long, wide mark, running right down it. "You've got a massive scratch. How did you do that?"

"No idea. Doesn't hurt." And he licked his finger and rubbed the long, straight mark. It faded. "All gone. Nothing serious."

Amanda nodded. "Good. Anyway, this afternoon—"

"You had sunstroke, Manda. Forget it," Grant interrupted. "And I'm dead beat, so if you're going to read, don't shine your torch my way, will you? Goodnight."

She sighed. "Goodnight."

The sleeping bag was cool and silky. Amanda snuggled down and opened the folklore book. Shining her torch on the pages and illustrations, she was soon engrossed in the story of the Battle of Endrith Valley.

"You'd be interested in this, Grant," Amanda called through the linen wall. "It's all about the battle that took place here. It was between the Endmore Clan and the Rithnoch Highlanders in 1314. Hundreds of men were killed. It says that sometimes, on the anniversary of the battle, people have reported hearing battle cries and the clash of swords echoing along the valley."

Grant didn't answer for a moment, and Amanda assumed that he was asleep. And then, quite softly, he said, "Maybe that's what you sensed this afternoon. Maybe you picked up on the vibes of the battle. You are a bit weird that way sometimes."

"I'm not weird!"

"Sensitive, then," Grant said. "You kind of sense things. Remember when Great Gran died? You felt funny all day. Remember, you kept on about going to visit her, and we'd only seen her the day before."

"I just *knew* something was wrong," Amanda murmured, remembering.

"And what about years ago, when I was on my

bike cycling down our pavement and you suddenly screamed at me to stop. I jammed my brakes on and had just screeched to a halt when that car came whizzing out of a drive. It would have hit me if you hadn't warned me. But you couldn't have seen it."

Amanda stared into the shadows. "I'd forgotten about that."

"Yeah, well. You were only about three. You were with Mum in the front garden. You couldn't have seen over the hedge."

"What does it mean, Grant?" Amanda whispered.

He suddenly poked his head around the dividing flap of linen, and grinned. "It means you're bonkers!"

She couldn't help but laugh. "Oh, go to sleep."

When Amanda awoke, dawn was breaking, allowing sunlight to dispel the shadows. She lay for a while, thinking. Then, stretching, she decided to get up and see if anyone was awake at the caravan.

Grant was sleeping like a log and so she moved quietly, so as not to waken him. Unzipping the outer tent, she stepped out onto the dewy, wet grass. It felt icy cold against her bare feet, but it didn't matter. It was a beautiful morning. The air was still cool and fresh, the sun just burning off the mists of daybreak. The loch was calm and tranquil.

High over the mountain a hawk soared, and from the forest came the dawn chorus of birdsong. Amanda breathed in the fresh Scottish air, throwing back her head as her eyes closed briefly against the hazy glare of early sunlight.

Then something hit her – like a blast of hot air. As if someone had just opened an oven door right into her face.

Her eyes sprang open.

Hot, rancid air continued to blast full into her face from nowhere. And something else…like a roar, a far distant, almost inaudible roar that seemed to come from a million miles away. It swept over her the same instant as the blast of hot, stale air.

Shocked, she stumbled backwards, tangling herself in the tent's guy ropes. Her startled eyes darted left and right. There was nothing to see, but her skin was prickling and the hairs at the nape of her neck were standing to attention.

Then, from the forest came an almighty shrieking, screaming din. And Amanda saw Rab Stewart come racing from the thicket, bony legs thudding like pistons on the ground, kilt swinging, arm raised as he raced towards her brandishing his walking stick.

Amanda gasped, then blinked…the sunlight was glinting off his stick, making it shine like steel.

He was running straight towards her, his eyes wild, his hair streaming out behind him, shouting at the top of his voice.

With a little shriek of her own, Amanda dived back into the tent and scrambled through to Grant. "Grant, wake up! Mr. Stewart's gone crazy – he's charging down here like a madman!"

"What…hey…wh—!"

"Get up!" Amanda yelled, tugging at his arm and yanking him out of bed just as pounding footsteps hared past their tent, accompanied by a long, loud shriek. "That's him!"

Grant scrambled out of his sleeping bag and together they stumbled to the open flaps of the tent and peered out.

Rab Stewart had run straight past the tent and was tearing off towards the mountain, his stick still raised in menace, shrieking at the top of his voice.

Grant burst out laughing. A moment later, the caravan door opened and their sleepy-eyed parents looked out, bewildered by all the shouting. They stared in astonishment at the sight of the flying Scotsman disappearing over the hill, still brandishing his stick.

"He's nuts!" Grant laughed. "Stark-raving bonkers!"

Their dad came wandering over, scratching his

head. "Am I seeing things, or was that old Mr. Stewart doing the three-minute mile?"

Grant was in stitches. "How could his knobbly old legs move that fast? He was like a streak of lightning. Incredible!"

"Oh, Lord. I thought we were here for some peace and quiet," Dad groaned, shaking his head. "Ah, well. Come on, you pair. Let's get the kettle on. An early breakfast is the only thing for it now."

Amanda linked her dad's arm, wishing she found it as funny as everyone else. But she couldn't get that first image of Rab Stewart from her head. When he first appeared from the forest, it hadn't been a stick he'd been brandishing at all.

It had been a sword.

Chapter Seven

After breakfast, no one seemed to want to wander far from the caravan. Dad busied himself sorting out his fishing gear, while Mum bustled about tidying up the caravan, which really didn't need tidying at all. Grant sat carving an animal shape from a chunk of wood, while Amanda tried to read, but found it impossible to concentrate.

Finally, Mum exclaimed, "What on Earth did the man think he was playing at?"

"Soldiers?" Amanda suggested. "Maybe he was re-enacting the battle?"

"Well, I wish he'd do his play-acting more quietly next time," Grant grumbled. "I'm going back to bed in a minute. I've only had half my sleep."

Nobody quite knew what to say to the old Scotsman when he visited later that morning.

"That was quite some run for an old timer this morning, Mr. Stewart," Dad remarked, raising his eyebrows.

"Aye, well, there's life in the old dog yet, y'know," he replied, his sharp pale eyes looking right at Amanda. "I hope I didn't startle you. When I'm out for an early-morning run, I tend to forget there might be people sleeping, and I get a little carried away at times with the shouting and the like."

"We thought you might be re-enacting the Battle of Endrith Valley," suggested Amanda.

"Aye, well, I can understand you thinking that, because we're just about to celebrate the anniversary of the great battle. Tomorrow's the actual day it all started." He lowered his voice, so that it was little more than a whisper and everyone had to crane their necks to hear what he had to say. "Some folk swear they've actually heard battle cries and swords clashing as day breaks."

"That's fascinating," Mum remarked, rubbing her arms. "The thought gives me goose bumps, though."

The old man fixed her with a penetrating stare. "If it worries you, then maybe you ought to move out of the valley to a more populated spot. Edinburgh's a beautiful city. You'd all enjoy spending your holiday there amongst the Edinburgh folk."

Safety in numbers, a voice in Amanda's head repeated. He was telling them to get out of here. He knew there was danger heading this way. Perhaps it was to do with the anniversary of the battle.

"We do actually plan on visiting Edinburgh," said her dad, looking slightly annoyed. "But that's on our way home. We certainly won't be scared off by stupid superstition. We fully intend staying put, right here in the valley, at least until the end of the week."

Amanda watched the old man, and saw him silently, barely noticeably, calculating on his fingers just how many days that was.

Looking steadily at him, she asked, "Do you think we'll hear those ghostly battle cries, Mr. Stewart?"

His bright eyes swivelled her way, seeming to spear right through her. He nodded his greying head. "Aye, I think *you* might."

Her dad jumped to his feet, startling everyone. He looked really angry now, but somehow managed to remain polite. "Well, it's been nice chatting to you again, but we mustn't keep you from... well, whatever it is you do."

"Aye, I'll be on my way," the old Scot said, taking the hint. But as he turned to go, his eyes met Amanda's again, fleetingly. He spoke directly to her. "But I'll not be far, if you should need me."

A cold shiver ran through her body. What was he telling her? She couldn't even begin to understand.

They all watched him stride away. When he was out of earshot, Dad shook his head in disbelief. "That old codger is a raving lunatic. I hope he didn't frighten anyone with that stupid ghost talk. The man should have more sense than to try and scare people."

"Oh, he's harmless," Mum said, trying to calm him down. "He's probably just lonely."

Amanda said nothing. She sat quietly as she tried to get her jumbled thoughts into order.

"I'll not be far, if you should need me."

If she needed him!

There *was* danger here. And he was trying to warn her. She stared after the thin, kilted figure marching off into the distance and knew that she had to get him to tell her everything. And the only way to do that was to speak to him again, soon – and alone.

When the day had returned to normal and everyone was engrossed in their own particular activity, with

Grant being taught fly-fishing by their dad and their mum adding a Scottish Highlander into the landscape painting she was working on, Amanda announced that she was going to see how many different types of fungi she could find.

She headed into the forest, feeling uneasy but knowing this was something she had to do. Ducking beneath branches and scrambling over fallen logs, she made a determined effort to note the way she was going so she didn't get lost again.

It was cool beneath the shelter of the trees – very little sunlight could penetrate the entwined branches overhead. But reaching a grassy clearing, the sun burst through and she immediately saw Rab Stewart's cottage.

It was quite small with just one square window and a narrow door. Its walls were made from cut pine. It also had a slated roof and a chimney. She blinked at the sight of it, amazed at finding it so easily, particularly as she and Grant had searched for hours yesterday. She really couldn't understand how they had missed it.

Oh, well. She'd found it now and, with any luck, old Mr. Stewart would be at home.

Sweeping aside the long feathery grasses, she picked her way towards the isolated cabin. She couldn't help but smile. It was like something from a fairy story. She almost expected the seven dwarfs to come marching out.

"Are you looking for me?" came a familiar voice and she swung round, startled to find the old Scotsman standing right next to her. "I'm sorry, I didn't mean to frighten you."

"No, it's all right," Amanda muttered, catching her breath. "I just didn't see you there."

"Like I said, I'm never far away…if you should need me."

She swallowed hard. "Yes…well, that's actually why I wanted to speak to you. What do you mean, *if we need you*? Are we in some kind of danger?"

For a second, he said nothing, and then softly murmured, "You already know you are."

Amanda went icy cold. "What sort of danger?" she breathed.

"You don't need to know, my wee hen. Just be warned, there's awful, terrible danger here for you, if you stay. You've got to persuade your family to move on. Get out of the valley. Once you're away from here, you'll not be bothered."

"Is it the battle? Ghosts can't hurt us, can they?"

He looked steadily at her. "No, *ghosts* can't hurt you."

"Then what danger are you talking about? I don't understand."

He sighed. "Ghosts can't touch you. But manifestations can."

"What? What's a manifestation?"

He held up his hands. "You're a wee bairn. I don't want to frighten you, but you must persuade your family to move on. You could camp out at Glenmoray. It's bonny there."

"But…"

His head tipped back, almost like an animal picking up a scent in the air. "I have to go. I've things to do."

"Not until you tell me what there is to be scared of!" Amanda said, defiantly standing in his way.

His eyes seemed to show their age for a second. Then, as if resigned, he whispered softly, "Beware the Beast."

Grant thought it the funniest thing he had heard all day. Rolling around on the grass, he hung on to his sides and warbled, "Och, aye, the beastie. It's coming to get us. We're doomed, all doomed!"

"Stop it, Grant!" Amanda said huffily. "I happen to believe him. I've felt something weird ever since we got here. This place is haunted by some horrible animal – a beast."

Still grinning, he sat cross-legged on the grass and looked up at her. "Manda, ghosts don't exist.

And if they did, they wouldn't be able to hurt you."

"No, but a manif—"

"Manda, he's nuts! A first-rate crackpot with a weird sense of humour. I bet he scares all the tourists with tales of the Beast. I suppose it makes a change from the Loch Ness Monster."

Dad wandered over, smiling. "And what's tickled our Grant?"

Grant told him about Mr. Stewart's Beast. Dad didn't find it amusing.

"That man!" he exploded. "He has no right scaring you like that. Amanda, I don't want you talking to him again. Do you hear me?"

"But, Dad! He's only trying to protect us. There's something here, something dangerous. He said we could camp out at Glenmoray and be safe—"

"Safe?" her dad raged. "He's the one who'll need protection if he carries on like this. The man's a lunatic. Now stay well away from him in future. Both of you!"

"But Dad—"

"No buts. Now back to the caravan. Your mother's made lunch and I don't want to hear another word about ghosts and beasts. Understood?"

As he marched back to the caravan, Amanda glared at her brother. "Thank you very much!"

Grant shrugged. "Okay, so he overreacted a bit. But you've got to admit, old Rabby does have a screw loose."

Frustrated and helpless, Amanda exclaimed, "Well, I hope you're right! I hope you're *all* right. Because if you're not, and he really is trying to give us a warming about some ghostly beast, which we're obviously all going to ignore, then we're in big trouble."

In the shadows of the cave, Karbel slunk low onto his belly, his yellow eyes burning with rage. Fury festered within him. He was wasting precious time being forced to flee by the old human. He needed to focus all his energies in manifesting himself, not wasting energy running and hiding.

That morning he had lain close by the humans' settlement, watching and waiting. Eventually, the young female had emerged as dawn broke. At first, she had not sensed his presence. She had not sensed him rising up from the grass to pad softly, silently, towards her. Not even when he was a breath away from her. Only when he had opened his jaws so wide that her head could easily have been devoured by one quick snap, had he been mortal, and he had roared directly into her face, *then*, and only then, had she sensed him.

If the old human had not come charging after him, he could have remained close, gathering strength from her fear, making himself strong and powerful...and mortal again.

But the old one had given chase, armed with his weapon, and human weapons were something to be afraid of. It had been because of a human's glinting steel dagger that his life had ended. He had to be careful. Perhaps they could wipe out his spirit life too. Yes, he would be careful. He would not make the same mistake twice. But soon now, he would take his revenge.

Very soon.

And he would relish the kill.

Chapter Eight

"I'm bored!" Grant complained, putting aside his penknife and the chunk of wood that was slowly becoming quite a work of art.

Amanda picked the carving up and turned it in her hand. "This is good, Grant. What is it? A dog?"

He shrugged. "Something like that. What do you fancy doing then, Manda? Hey, I know. Let's get our torches and investigate that cave again."

Amanda shot him a disbelieving look. "Brilliant, Grant! We've just been warned about some ghostly beast, and you want to explore a dark prehistoric cave!"

He grinned. "It's daytime. Ghosts don't come

out in the day. Everyone knows that."

"That's a fact, is it?"

"Come on, Manda. You can't let that old crackpot spoil our holiday."

"That *crackpot* is trying to protect us," Amanda stated determinedly.

"So we sit here around the caravan for the rest of the week? I don't think so. *I'm* going to investigate that cave. *You* can stay here, if you like."

Amanda jumped to her feet as her brother headed towards their tent and chased after him. "Aren't you even a bit worried that there's something out to hurt us?"

Grant strode on and ducked inside the tent, where he threw a few things into his backpack. "Nope! Manda, that Rabby Stewart is a fruitcake. I'll see you later."

Amanda could see he was determined, and the last thing she wanted was for her brother to go off alone. If there was danger, it was better if they faced it together.

Safety in numbers.

"Hang on." She sighed. "I'll come with you."

Grant turned and grinned. "Good."

It was easy to find the cave, particularly with Grant leading the way. Amanda wished for once that his sense of direction would let him down and they wouldn't be able to find it again. But, suddenly, there it was. An eerie, dark hole set deep in the base of the mountain – ominous and foreboding.

"Can you imagine cave men living here, Manda? And woolly mammoths and giant bears and sabre-toothed tigers?"

"In this country?" she exclaimed in disbelief.

"Absolutely. I am talking tens of thousands of years ago. Like in the Ice Age, when creatures could have travelled from one continent to another on the ice floes."

He was right, Amanda realized as she clambered over the boulders towards the cave's entrance. In her thoughts, she could almost conjure up a picture of life in those prehistoric days. This could indeed have been the home of primitive people. Perhaps a tribe of early Highland settlers who would clothe themselves in animal skins, feed their families with the meat from animals they hunted down and build their fires to ward off dangerous predators.

She heard a scream.

A terrified, high-pitched cry, which came and went like the blinking of an eye. But which shook her to the core.

The scream had come from inside her own head.

"Keep up, Manda!" Grant shouted down as he

reached the cave entrance.

It's just the sun, she told herself, trembling slightly. Too much sun.

"Manda! You okay?"

She shook herself and called back. "Grant, I really don't fancy going in there. How about we try to find Mr. Stewart's cottage? I'm sure I'll remember the way this time."

"And disobey Dad's orders?" he remarked, raising one eyebrow.

"I know, but I just don't think we ought to be messing about in horrible caves…"

He hadn't heard. Already he had been swallowed up by the cave's foreboding blackness.

Amanda had no choice but to follow.

She heard his voice as she reached the entrance.

"Hellooo! Anyone home?" His words echoed around the cave. Followed by a deathly silence.

All Amanda could hear was the thudding of her heart.

Her brother reappeared, grinning. "No one home. Shall we go in?"

"No, I really don't fancy it, Grant. It's pitch-black in there—"

"Stop whingeing and come on," he said, going back in.

Reluctantly, Amanda followed. At least if she

kept close to Grant she could keep an eye on him and stop him from doing anything dangerous. Although she soon saw that there wasn't much he could do. Sweeping her torch around the cave, she saw that was all it was. A deep cave with a cold, sandy floor and a few big rocks and boulders. No potholes, no monsters…no beasts.

Grant shone his torch at the walls near the back of the cave. "Hey, Manda, there really are some cave drawings. Come and look. There are scratchings of people, see? And creatures with tusks or something. Told you there were mammoths in prehistoric times."

"Doesn't look much like a mammoth to me. It's more like a big dog or something."

"With tusks?"

"Perhaps they're not tusks. Perhaps they're teeth."

He followed his torchlight along the wall. "Oh, wow! This is brilliant."

Despite her fears, Amanda had to agree. She had never seen real cave drawings before. They were very faint, not much more than scratched stick-drawings, but they clearly showed people and large animals.

Fascinated, she wandered slowly around the cave, lost in thought about the people who had drawn these images thousands of years ago. Grant brushed against her and she turned, expecting to find him looking over her shoulder. To her surprise, he was at the far side of the cave.

"Did you just brush past me?"

"Me? No."

"Oh," she murmured, distinctly feeling something again. Something soft and faint, almost like a warm breeze. "I thought you did. Can't you feel it every now and then, like a fluttering?"

"Yeah, I felt something like that earlier. It's probably a breeze from somewhere," Grant said vaguely, still engrossed in what he was looking at. "Although...actually...a couple of minutes ago I felt a blast of hot air. Don't know where that came from. Just a big blast, right into my face."

Amanda suddenly remembered what had happened to her that morning. "Grant, listen...just before Mr. Stewart came charging down the valley this morning, I felt a hot blast of air in my face too. All smelly and horrible."

"This was smelly," said Grant. "I suppose there could be tunnels that go really deep underground. It could be hot air coming up from the bowels of the Earth. Anyway, I've seen enough. Ready to go?"

"Oh, yes. Definitely!" Amanda eagerly agreed. And, as they emerged into the sunshine, she added, "It *was* really interesting, Grant. I'm glad you persuaded me."

"See, big brother knows best."

Amanda raised her eyebrows. "Well, big brother won't be in Mum's good books when she sees what you've done to your T-shirt."

"Why?" he asked, looking down at himself.

"It's all snagged. Look, you've got threads hanging off all over the place."

"Oh, no! This is my best T-shirt. How did I do that?"

"You must have rubbed against some rough rock. Look, your arms are all scratched, too."

He licked his finger and tried to rub the scratch marks off his skin as he'd done before. But they remained. Long, straight, white scratches on his suntanned arms. The snagged T-shirt was definitely irreparable.

As they walked back down to the valley, still examining the T-shirt, Karbel padded after them, emerging from the shadows of the cave into the sunlight. He leaped effortlessly onto a high boulder, stretched out in the warm sunshine and watched them go.

At last, he could feel the heat of the sun on his body again. How wonderful it felt after so long.

He curled and unfurled his front paws like a cat and purred contentedly at the sight of the threads that still clung to his long, razor-sharp claws.

At last, it was happening.

"Okay, I give up! Where's old Scotty's cottage?" Grant demanded.

Amanda stood in the forest clearing, positive that this was the place she'd discovered Rab Stewart's cottage. She looked around in frustration. "But it was here! Honestly, Grant, I know I've got my directions right this time. It was right here!"

Her brother stared at her, eyebrows arched. "Yeah, course it was."

Amanda swept aside the long feathery grasses and wandered closer to where she thought the cottage should have been.

Grant walked alongside, smiling at her like she was stupid. "Manda. How I wish you had a sense of direction. How you are ever going to get through life, I do not know!"

"Oh, shut up!" she exclaimed, frustrated and annoyed with herself for getting it wrong. Yet she was positive she'd come to the right spot. "I don't believe this. The cabin was here. It *was*!"

Grant looked down at the ground. "Manda, we've been here before. Look, it's those slippery slates we came across the other day."

Frowning, Amanda scuffed some moss off the slates. "These could be from a roof. Look, there's a stone base, like a floor."

"No bricks from the walls though," said Grant.

"He had wooden walls – cut-pine logs," Amanda said softly.

"There's a charred bit here," Grant said, examining the area further. "Could have been a fireplace."

"The cabin had a chimney," she breathed, as an icy shiver ran through her veins. "Grant…"

He glanced up.

In barely a whisper, she said, "This is it. This is Rab Stewart's cabin."

He frowned. "But I thought you'd found a real cottage. Not just old remains."

"I did," she breathed. "I saw it standing. It looked really nice – like something from a fairy tale. This is all that's left of it."

Grant gave her an odd glance. "Fairy tale is the right description if you ask me. This has been derelict for ever. Look at all the weeds smothering it. There's years of undergrowth here."

"I know," she murmured, trying to rub away the spiky little goose bumps that suddenly erupted over her arms. "I know that."

Grant stared at her, then raised his eyebrows. "Manda, have you had too much sun again?"

She said nothing to her parents that night. They wouldn't have approved of them going looking for Mr. Stewart's cabin after all that had been said. So that evening over dinner, they chatted about the cave drawings, and planned how they would spend the next day.

Amanda didn't think she would be able to sleep. There was so much going on in her head. Yet, as soon as her head hit the pillow, she was fast asleep. However, her dreams were fitful and strange and she woke again as dawn began to break. Almost instantly she felt herself break out into a cold sweat.

Something was just outside the tent again, only this time she didn't just sense it. This time she could actually *hear* it.

The sound of grass being crushed underfoot.

Footsteps – human, animal? She couldn't tell. Just slow, menacing footsteps. Something was taking its time, stalking, circling...

"Mr. Stewart...is that you?" Amanda whispered, her voice almost refusing to work, hoping desperately to hear his familiar voice saying, "Aye, lass. It's only me."

But all she heard was the soft crushing of grass

as someone, or something, moved stealthily around the tent.

Beware the Beast... A Scottish voice echoed in her head.

Was there a beast outside?

What kind of beast?

Oh, there are bound to be deer and otters...

"Grant, wake up!" she cried, terror forcing her into action as she reached under the flap to shake her brother awake.

"What? Huh!"

"Something's outside," she hissed. "Listen!"

"Oh, Manda. Not again!"

"You *must* be able to hear that. Listen, will you!"

Grant fell silent, as if holding his breath. Then, he quietly got out of bed, reached for his torch and crawled towards the outer tent zip. There was a determined look on his face. Amanda swallowed hard, her heart thudding against her ribcage.

He had heard. This time he knew she wasn't imagining it. And he was ready.

"There's something out there all right," he whispered. "And it's big..."

Her blood ran cold. She already knew that, she just didn't want to believe it. "Perhaps it's a deer," she whispered, knowing it wasn't.

"No, listen…" Grant murmured. "That's not a deer. A deer would be light-footed. This is something big…something heavy."

He looked white in the morning's light. Amanda stared at him, desperately needing reassurance. "Like what? A fox? A wolf?"

"Bigger," he breathed. "Much bigger."

"Bear?" she could hardly say the word. Her throat and lips were parched with fear.

"Possibly," Grant murmured, moving stealthily, unzipping the outer tent just enough to peer through.

Amanda hung back. "Can you see anything?"

"Nothing…ugh! What was that?"

"What?" Amanda cried in alarm, looking out, trying to see what had startled him.

"That blast of hot air again, right in my face."

"Let me see," Amanda said, unzipping the flap a little more and peering warily outside, half expecting to come face to face with a monstrous animal.

But there was nothing to see, and they both crept out of the tent and stood looking all around. A pale grey morning mist shrouded the valley like a cloud fallen from the sky. Stillness and silence lay over the Valley of Shadows.

Except for the distant drumbeat.

Far, far away there was a drummer, beating out a solid marching rhythm.

And then accompanying it came the sound of bagpipes, wailing out a mournful tune.

"I can hear a marching band somewhere," Amanda whispered, amazed that anyone would be playing so early.

Grant tilted his head to one side. "I can't hear it."

Amanda cast him an odd glance. "Got cotton wool in your ears?"

"No," he replied, meeting her gaze with a confused look. "There's not a sound out here."

Amanda frowned. She could definitely hear a drumbeat and bagpipes. But there were more sounds now, too. Strange, faraway sounds, almost like people shouting. Like a distant hubbub of voices.

"You must be able to hear it. Listen, Grant. It's coming from the valley."

"What is? I can't hear a thing."

Amanda swung round and faced him, her frown heavy over her eyes. "Are you deaf or what? There are people coming this way…I can hear an enormous crowd of people heading right towards us. And horses, can't you hear those hoof beats? Can't you feel the vibrations through the ground?"

Grant slowly shook his head. "Manda, it's as silent as the grave out here."

Amanda suddenly realized he wasn't joking, and

a feeling of panic tightened her throat. Her eyes widened as the rising wall of sound grew louder.

"Shouting! They're shouting now!" She gripped Grant's arm. "And screaming. Grant, there are people screaming." Her voice rose. "Can't you hear those screams, those horrible shrieks? Like…like people killing each other."

Grant put his arm around her. "We'd better go and get Mum."

But Amanda just clung to him, tears welling up in her eyes as the screaming continued to ring out, echoing all across the valley.

"What's happening, Grant? What's happening to me?"

"It's okay, Manda. It's okay," he tried to reassure her. "You're probably not fully awake, you might be sleepwalking – you might be in the middle of a dream."

"Pinch me, then," she cried, clasping her hands over her ears. "Grant, I can hear swords clashing. Swords and screams. It's right here, all around us. Make them stop! Make them go away!"

He held her tightly and pulled her back into the tent. "It's okay, Manda. It's okay," he said, trying to calm her. "There's no one there. It's just echoes."

"Echoes from the past," Amanda said, knowing exactly what she was listening to. These were sounds from centuries past. She recalled the words from the folklore book.

Sometimes, on the anniversary of the battle, people have reported hearing battle cries and the clash of swords echoing along the valley.

"The battle…" Amanda murmured, looking at Grant with tearful eyes. "The book said that some people could hear the sound of the battle."

"And you're sensitive enough to be one of those people," Grant answered.

She nodded.

"Can you still hear it?" he asked softly.

Amanda nodded. "Horses whinnying, men shouting, swords crashing."

Grant led her to the corner of the tent and they sat, arms around each other, saying nothing, until finally daylight broke through, and the sound of a battle that had raged hundreds of years before slowly drifted back into the past from where it had escaped.

Chapter Nine

From a rocky mountain ridge, Karbel gazed down into the valley. All was calm again. The battle between the humans had slipped back between the layers of time once more. On so many hot summer mornings over the centuries he had witnessed the scene. And always the same outcome. Mankind killing mankind.

He didn't understand the reasoning behind the slaughter. But then humans were strange creatures. They used weapons to slay each other. He would always steer clear of human's weapons, whether he was mortal or of the spirit world. Their daggers might destroy his spirit as easily as one had destroyed his body. And that he could not risk.

So, throughout the long day, he remained high on his ridge, continuing to amass the strength he needed to become mortal again.

And his goal was close. His manifestation was gathering momentum. That very morning he had felt the dew-soaked grass beneath his paws as he circled the humans' tent. Had it not been for the commotion of the battle he could have drawn power from their fear.

But the human spirits returning to repeat their senseless slaughter had been too much to endure. Especially as the old warrior was there yet again. Once more, Karbel had been forced to flee back to the safety of the mountains, and watch until it was over.

Now, in the distance, he saw the two young humans. The male had a small weapon in his hand. Karbel could see the sunlight glinting off the steel. A low growl sounded from his throat as he focused more intensely.

The male was carving an image. Karbel hissed in rage as he saw what it was.

It was an image of his own kind.

So that was his plan! To create a small image of Karbel – and then what?

Destroy it? Throw it into a fire?

Destroy his spirit by burning a carved likeness?

"No!" Karbel threw back his head and howled in rage. No, that would not happen! The young male had to die. Now. This day, before he could complete his carving.

Summoning up all his spiritual strength, Karbel focused all his might and power on becoming mortal again. And as his mortality increased, his belly grumbled. How long since he had eaten? Since he had tasted warm flesh?

Decades.

Usually, there was little reason to exhaust himself by manifesting himself back into the mortal world. He was content in spirit form.

Usually.

Only when something disturbed his spiritual existence, like now, with the arrival of the young male who had slain him millennia ago. And who had returned to destroy his spirit.

But soon he would taste blood and flesh again.

Very soon.

With a burst of energy, he rose up and stretched his long, lithe body. Then, he sprang determinedly forwards, leaping down the mountainside, pouncing from boulder to boulder, ridge to ridge. Zigzagging his way down the rock face until he was standing, paw-deep in lush, green, valley grass.

He moved as gracefully as a cat, loping along the curve of loch, his massive paws now making faint imprints on the earth, crushing the grass as he moved stealthily ever nearer to his prey.

Close by, a small grey rabbit raised its head, bright eyes blinking in fright, ears twitching. For a moment it stood motionless, sensing danger approaching, but seeing nothing, except for what looked like a shimmering heat haze moving along the edge of the loch.

Alarmed, the little creature scuttled off into longer grass, frightened, but with no idea what it was frightened of.

Karbel padded on, quickening his pace as he saw the two young humans head off towards the forest. Now he could smell them. Their scent filled his nostrils, while saliva gathered around his black gums and dripped from the corners of his mouth. As he padded on, a drop of his saliva landed on a blade of grass.

Like a dewdrop, it glistened there for anyone to see.

Amanda had been glad that their parents had suggested a day trip. They'd visited nearby villages and wandered around quaint old shops. But both she and Grant had been quiet, so much so that their parents had asked what was wrong.

Amanda desperately wanted to tell them. But she knew they would dismiss the battle sounds as imagination. So what was the point?

As they drove back into the valley, Amanda felt a growing unease. She peered through the car window, looking...searching. Although she didn't quite know what she expected to see.

While Mum prepared the evening meal and Grant sat quietly whittling away at his carving, Amanda came up with a suggestion.

"We need to talk to Rab Stewart again, Grant," she whispered, making sure their parents didn't overhear. "I'm sure he would understand about the battle sounds. And I want him to explain about the beast. I want *you* to hear what he has to say."

"And how do we find him? His cottage is derelict, isn't it?"

Amanda shrugged helplessly. "I don't know. I don't understand it at all. I suppose I must have made a mistake with the location – mustn't I?"

Grant shrugged. "You hear people who aren't here. Maybe you saw a cottage that isn't real, too."

"But Mr. Stewart *is* real," Amanda stressed. "We've all seen him. Please, Grant. Let's go and see if we can find him."

To her surprise, he needed little persuasion.

"Okay," Grant said, putting the carving and penknife into his pocket as he got to his feet. He called to their mum. "How long till dinner, Mum?"

"About an hour," came her reply from inside the caravan.

"Manda and I are going for a walk. We won't be long."

"Okay then!"

They set off, walking away from the caravan, up past their tent and into the forest. But once again the log cabin was nowhere to be seen. All they found was that same pile of rubble. No sign of the old Scotsman at all.

Finally, they emerged from the forest into a part of the valley they hadn't explored before. Immediately, Amanda began to feel edgy.

"We'd better head back," she said, glancing over her shoulder.

Grant looked at his watch. "Suppose so. Are you going to sleep in the caravan tonight?"

"Are you?"

"Nah! You ought to, though."

"No, I don't want to leave you on your own," Amanda said, looking back over her shoulder again. She couldn't shake the unnerving feeling that something or someone was behind them.

"Me?" he puzzled. "I'm okay. It's you…and why do you keep looking back? Can you hear something?"

Her skin was starting to prickle. "Not *hear* exactly, it's just a feeling."

"We'll get a move on then, shall we? After I've answered a call of nature…"

"Oh, Grant! Can't you wait?" Amanda complained, wishing they were back at the caravan now. Wishing they hadn't come so far.

"Two ticks," Grant announced, disappearing once more into the trees.

Amanda waited, goose bumps erupting all over her body, unable to shake the horrible, sense of foreboding.

"Come on, come on," she muttered to herself, wishing Grant would hurry up. The sun was low in the sky now, turning blue to gold and casting long shadows across the ground.

She walked on a little, knowing Grant would easily catch her up, but still she couldn't stop looking back, the awful feeling that something was following them continuing to make her skin prickle.

Grant finally reappeared.

"At last!" Amanda exclaimed in relief. "Now, can we get back to the caravan?"

He strolled away from the shade of the trees into

the bright evening sunlight, the sun casting his shadow across the ground behind him.

Amanda was about to walk on when she saw it.

Another shadow, grotesque and immense, slinking just behind him.

Stalking him.

The shadow of a creature with a sunken, curved spine, a low belly and a massive, misshapen head.

She froze. And then a cloud passed over the sun and the shadows were gone.

Struck dumb, Amanda stood riveted with shock. Expecting *something* to prowl into view at any second. But nothing emerged from the forest behind her unsuspecting brother.

No monster, no grotesque beast.

"Manda? What's up with you? You're as white as a ghost."

"I...I thought I saw something."

"What sort of something?"

Her throat felt parched with fear. "The shadow of an animal, following you out of the forest."

Grant spun round. "I didn't see anything. Tell you what, though – I didn't half scratch my back on some brambles."

"Did you? Let me see," Amanda murmured, trying not to let panic take hold. The light here in the valley played tricks. It was renowned for it. The

Valley of Shadows – that's what people called it.

But, as she looked at her brother's back, she gasped. "Oh, Grant!"

"What?"

"What on Earth did you do? You've got three huge scratches right down the back of your T-shirt. It's ruined, much worse than your other one. Three straight lines from the top of your shoulder right down to your waist." She traced the lines with her hand and Grant winced.

"Ouch! That's sore."

"Here, let me have a better look," she said, lifting the back of his T-shirt up. She gasped. The scratches had cut through the fabric to his skin. And at his shoulder, where the scratches seemed to have started, were three drops of blood. "You're bleeding."

"Ah, it's nothing," he shrugged, wriggling his T-shirt back into place.

"How can you say it's nothing?" Amanda exclaimed, frightened now. "We had an animal creeping round our tent last night. Then I saw the shadow of...of *something*. And now you've got scratches down your back!"

"Manda, they're just scratches. The forest is full of sharp twigs."

Unconvinced, and growing more panicky by

the second, she said sarcastically, "Really? Three equally spaced twigs that scratched you from your shoulder down to your waist, like this…" As she argued, she drew her fingers down through the air – like claws.

Instantly, she turned icy cold. Softly, she whispered, "Those scratches were made by an animal."

"Don't be daft. I'd have seen it."

"Mr. Stewart said that we should beware the beast."

Grant laughed. "Yeah, some ghostly animal. Amanda, ghosts can't hurt you or we'd have been chopped to pieces in that ghostly battle this morning."

"No, but manifestations can. That's what Mr. Stewart said."

Grant stopped laughing and the colour drained completely from his face. He looked almost sick.

"What does 'manifestation' mean?" Amanda whispered.

"It means *real*," he breathed, taking her arm and striding out towards camp. "It means becoming real. Taking on human or living form."

Amanda felt her skin begin to prickle. "A ghost becoming real?"

"Sounds stupid, doesn't it," he said shakily.

Amanda felt her throat constrict with fear. "Yes, really stupid...how far to the caravan?"

"Not far," he said, trying to sound normal. "Just over the brow of that hill, I reckon. We'll get a move on, shall we?"

"Yes," she agreed, fighting off the sickly sensation of fear that had settled in her stomach.

Her brother's calm exterior didn't fool her and as they lengthened their stride she checked over her shoulder, not really expecting to see anything that hadn't been there a second before. But to her horror, there was something there now. It looked like a heat haze – an odd swirling patch of shimmering light a short distance behind them.

She turned away, concentrating on where she was going, squeezing her eyes shut for a second to try and clear what she hoped was a blur brought on by the intense light of the sunset.

She had to look back again. It was still there. Just a hazy mass which seemed to be keeping pace with them.

"What's that just behind us, Grant?" she muttered, her throat constricting so badly she could barely form the words.

He glanced back and immediately stumbled. Amanda steadied him as he continued walking half backwards, unable to take his eyes off what he was seeing.

Or almost seeing.

"I don't know, it's weird. Must be a reflection from the loch, or a heat haze or something."

"You don't think it looks a bit like an animal?" Amanda croaked, holding on to Grant's arm as they broke into an uneasy jog.

"Nah, it's a trick of the light. It's nothing."

She looked over her shoulder again. "I don't like it."

"It's nothing. Keep calm. Just concentrate on getting up this hill without falling over. We should be able to see the caravan from there."

But Amanda couldn't help turning round. To her horror, the haze was definitely taking on a shape.

"I'm scared."

"Keep going. Don't look back, just keep going."

But it was impossible not to look, and turning her head once more Amanda could quite clearly see the distinct shape of an animal.

A huge animal, prowling behind them, moving with the stealth of a panther. Only it was bigger than a panther, much bigger.

Beware the beast.

"Grant, it's the beast!" Amanda cried, stumbling.

Grant stopped her from falling. "No, it's not! It's

a trick of the light. Just keep running."

"But it is! It's the beast that Mr. Stewart warned us about. Look!"

They both glanced back. Now there was no mistaking the definite shimmering form of a huge animal. It was immense and horrific and, whichever world it belonged to, it wasn't this one.

Yet it *was* here and it was loping after them, keeping pace without effort.

Grant muttered something under his breath and then grabbed hold of Amanda's wrist. "Run, Manda! And, whatever you do, don't fall over."

Chapter Ten

Karbel gave chase. It was an easy chase – his powerful body was made for speed. Mortal or immortal. His long strides gathered pace to keep his prey within striking distance. He was playing with them.

Like frightened gazelles, the two young humans sprinted ahead of him. As they ran up the hill, he could hear their gasping breath. He could smell their sweat mingling with their fear.

Karbel absorbed it, fed on it, felt their terror giving him strength – the final boost of strength that would bring him to full manifestation.

He knew he would not be able to sustain mortality for long. It was too draining. He needed to live just long enough to destroy these two young humans – as he should have done centuries ago.

He kept pace with them, just a stride behind. They looked back over their shoulders constantly, terror in their faces.

Karbel revelled in the game. Like cat and mouse, he quickened his pace, closing the gap, his excitement rising as they tried to outrun him. Adrenaline rushing through his veins, Karbel sprang at the humans as they reached the brow of the hill, his half-spirit and half-mortal presence bowling them over.

They screamed and rolled halfway down the hill before scrambling to their feet again.

Ahead of them now, Karbel spun around and faced them so that they ran straight through him, crying out as they tangled with his spirit form. He sucked in their terror and confusion – it added substance to his shimmering form.

He stood, dripping saliva, as they fled down the hill towards their camp. He let them go for a moment and then, snarling with sheer, malevolent pleasure, he continued the chase.

"We can do it, Mand," Grant gasped, still gripping

her wrist and dragging her. "Don't stop, k[...]
There's the caravan...not far...just keep ru[...]

Winded from being bowled over by the b[...]
sick from the awful sensation as they had tangled
with its thick, cold, intangible substance, which
reeked of evil, she gasped, "It's toying with us.
Playing until it's ready for the kill."

"It's not going to kill us!" Grant shouted. "Just
keep going...we're nearly there."

"I can't see Mum and Dad."

"Straight into the tent, then."

"But that's no protection!" Amanda cried, her
lungs burning now with the exertion. She realized
that Grant was in the same state.

"I've got to stop...need to catch my breath."

But they tore on, Amanda with a burning stitch
in her side, Grant gasping for breath. And all the
while the beast kept pace, enjoying the cruel chase.

Somehow they reached the tent and dived inside
just as a great blast of energy swept by. Grant
collapsed onto his knees, drawing in huge lungfuls of
air. Amanda doubled up, gripping her sides until the
burning sensation eased.

"Mum and Dad have *got* to believe this,"
she gasped.

"Too right," Grant panted. "Soon as we've got
our breath back, we'll run like mad to the caravan

and tell them everything. Then we'll pack up and go. Okay?"

"Okay," Amanda agreed. Then anxiously she asked, "Do you think it's still there, waiting for us?"

Right on cue, she had her answer. The tent lurched to one side as if a great weight had pushed against it.

She huddled closer to her brother. "What are we going to do?"

He said nothing, but his expression took on a harder, more determined look. He took his penknife from his pocket and opened the blade.

"What use…" She stopped herself from asking how effective the knife would be against a massive beast that wasn't even mortal. Instead, she picked up a torch. Like the penknife, it wasn't much of a weapon, but it was better than nothing.

Crouched, ready to run or to fight, they bided their time, listening as the beast circled the tent, waiting for the right moment to make their dash. But then came the sound.

A roar. At first it seemed distant and Amanda immediately recalled the other morning when hot air had blasted into her face. Now she knew what it was. Only this time the roar grew stronger, louder, as if it were being summoned up from the depths of hell.

It was followed by a furious clawing at the sides

of the tent. At first, there were just long indentations of claw marks down the nylon fabric, then as the beast's anger raged the indentations became snags and rips.

"The tent's not going to hold it at bay," Grant exclaimed.

"Grant, watch out!" Amanda screamed. "It's trying to force its way through the side of the tent!"

Mesmerized, they watched in horror as the beast pushed its head into the fabric of the tent. The nylon stretched tighter, moulding itself to every contour and feature of its monstrous face.

Amanda and Grant stared in disbelief.

"It can't be," Grant said in a hushed breath.

Amanda shuffled, terrified, away from the sight taking shape before her eyes. It was clear what it was. The two long, curved fangs confirmed that this creature was not of this world. Not any longer.

This beast should have vanished from the Earth thousands of years ago.

The sabre-toothed tiger was a creature from the distant past.

Chapter Eleven

Grant grabbed Amanda's arm, his grip like steel, his eyes huge. "We've got to get out of here. It'll rip its way through the tent in no time."

"But where? The caravan?"

"No, we'll never make it. We wouldn't stand a chance...sorry, Manda," he added, seeing her horrified expression. "The forest's our best chance. If we could hide just long enough for it to lose sight of us, then we could make a dash to the caravan. Quick, while it's still trying to get in. It might not see us if we creep out really quietly." He put his finger to his lips. "Don't even breathe."

They slunk out of the tent, crouching low, and crept around the side furthest away from the beast.

In a moment, they were amongst the shade and cover of the forest – and they ran. Warily at first, then picking up speed, they raced as fast as the undergrowth would allow them, trampling over dead wood, leaping fallen branches, being snagged and torn on brambles.

Amanda glanced back over her shoulder, expecting *it* to be there, but thankfully there was no sign. They raced on, desperately trying to get as far away from the beast as possible. Amanda kept on until her chest hurt and her lungs screamed for oxygen.

"Grant, I need to stop…"

He snatched a quick look at her face, then pulled her down behind a fallen tree trunk that was smothered in moss and fungi. He was gasping for breath too. As he collapsed in a heap beside her, something fell from his pocket.

The wooden carving that he'd been whittling these last few days. Amanda stared at it in horror.

"Grant – look at what you've carved!"

He picked it up and stared at it. "I don't know how that happened, it started off as a fox…it just sort of took on that shape."

Amanda continued staring in horror, a sick feeling growing inside. "It…it's a sabre-toothed tiger! Grant, you've carved a sabre-toothed tiger!"

The colour had drained from his face. "I didn't intend to, Mand…you don't think I've conjured it up, do you?"

"I don't know," she breathed. "Anything's possible."

Grant got to his knees and fumbled in his pocket for his knife. "In that case, if I created this monster, I can just as easily get rid of it."

Flipping open the blade, he placed the wooden carving on a flat stone and hacked it in half. The two pieces slid off the stone, and Grant turned hopefully to Amanda.

"Think it's done the trick?"

"I hope so," she said, glancing back the way they'd come. But what she saw sent her hopes plummeting. "Oh, no! Look!"

He swung around.

They both saw the movement – a patch of long grass parting as if an invisible force was pushing its way through.

But it was no illusion. A massive shimmering form prowled silently between the long, feathery grasses. A swaying, sauntering entity,looking almost as if it were carved from glass. A creature as deadly and dangerous as when it walked the Earth millennia ago.

The beast.

They cowered lower, but Amanda knew there was no hope of remaining undetected. It would pick up their scent – smell their fear.

She clung to Grant. He was gripping his penknife so hard his knuckles had turned white. His body was tense and rigid, his steely grey eyes fixed on the prowling beast, while she trembled so badly the ferns and twigs around her rustled softly.

The prehistoric creature padded closer, all the while its shimmering form coming more into focus, taking on more and more substance. Its sabre fangs glinting as shafts of evening sunlight streaked down between the trees.

The cracking of dead wood beneath its massive paws showed how the beast's strength and power were growing by the second. It was the only sound to be heard in the forest. The birds had ceased their chirping. Even the insects had become still.

The beast slunk closer, as if choosing the right direction, the right moment to make its attack. And then it halted. It raised its grotesque head, picking up their scent in the air, then turned to where Amanda and Grant hid, its menacing, glittering eyes piercing the undergrowth to where they cowered.

Amanda's heart banged against her ribcage.

The beast narrowed its eyes, then, opening its immense jaws, let out a roar that sent the birds shrieking and flapping in panic into the air.

And then silence descended once again.

"Grant…" Amanda breathed, trembling as she clung on to her brother's arm. But he began to ease himself free of her grip. Very slowly getting to his feet. Emerging from their pathetic hideaway. "Grant? What are you doing? Get down!" Amanda hissed, horrified that there was no way the beast could fail to see them now.

"So you want a fight, do you?" Grant said.

"No!" Amanda cried, dragging at Grant's T-shirt, desperately trying to pull him down out of sight.

But her brother stood tall, facing the beast, penknife slightly raised in defiance.

The beast stood its ground, its cruel eyes fixed upon Grant as if he were the prey it had waited a long, long time to confront.

Grant raised his arm, ready to do battle. It was a puny gesture against the massive, powerful creature.

"Don't," Amanda whimpered, still cowering behind the fallen log, wishing she felt as brave as her brother. Wishing their dad was here.

"I'll try and hold him off, Manda," Grant murmured, his shoulders set squarely. "You backtrack and find Dad."

"No, I'm not leaving you here with this… this thing."

"Just get out of here, Manda. Just run and keep running. The caravan's that way," he said, jerking his head to the left. "It can't chase both of us at the same time. And I think, by the way it's looking, it's me it's after."

Amanda didn't move. She was shaking so badly there was no strength in her legs to run for help anyway. But she couldn't leave her brother. She would never do that.

Her terror rose as the beast, with its glittering eyes still fixed on Grant, sat back slowly on its powerful hind legs as if preparing to launch itself at them. A low snarling sound rolled out from its slavering jaws.

"Run, Manda!" Grant yelled. "Get back to the caravan, get Dad. If this thing wants a fight then it can have one."

Panic gripped her and she screamed, "Help us! Somebody please help us!"

From nowhere, Rab Stewart came storming through the trees, kilt flying, brandishing his stick, and yelling at the top of his voice.

Grant staggered. "Where did he come from?"

If you need me, just call.

"Mr. Stewart, watch out! It's the beast!" Amanda screamed.

But he knew.

He knew the beast was there. Hadn't he warned them enough times?

"Run, you two!" Rab Stewart yelled, as he launched himself fearlessly at the snarling sabre-toothed tiger. "Get out of here! Run for your lives!"

But Amanda and Grant stood mesmerized as Rab Stewart raised his arm and, instead of his gnarled old stick, a steely Highland sword flashed in the fading sunlight.

"He's got a sword!" Grant gasped.

Amanda's eyes were like saucers. "I know," she whispered.

Rab Stewart's movements were quick and agile. He handled his sword like a warrior. Showing no sign of age now, he darted left and right, ducking, lunging, avoiding the beast's vicious attack as the creature snapped and clawed and fought back for all it was worth.

Again and again Rab Stewart thrust his sword at the creature, but the two opponents seemed evenly matched. Somehow, Rab avoided the evil claws and fangs of the beast, while the animal in turn leaped and pranced to avoid the killing edge of Rab's sword.

Amanda was trembling, holding on to Grant for support as her knees weakened at the sight of the terrifying battle. The snarling and spitting from the beast mixed with Rab's war cries and the thud of his sword as it missed its target and slammed into the earth – all echoed agonizingly through the forest.

Then, suddenly, the beast lashed out and caught Rab Stewart a terrible blow, sending him sprawling onto the ground.

"Mr. Stewart!" Amanda screamed as the beast pounced onto the spot where he had fallen.

"I've got to help him!" Grant yelled, leaping over the fallen log before Amanda could stop him.

"Grant!" Amanda screamed in terror.

A terrified, high-pitched cry.

But like her brother, she couldn't just stand and watch. Snatching up the nearest broken branch, she stumbled over the log and raced after him.

Grant's arm was raised. He looked fearless. Every fibre of his being showed determination and bravery. For a second, the sight of her brother going in to fight the ghostly demon left her breathless. But she knew he was no match for this monster.

Grant was armed with nothing but a feeble penknife. Yet, as he charged towards the beast, its small steel blade glinted in the evening sunlight. And it no longer looked like a cheap penknife.

It looked like a Highland warrior's dagger.

A dagger pointing straight at the beast's heart.

Chapter Twelve

Karbel had heard it. Amanda's terrified scream.

A high-pitched scream of terror and warning that echoed right across the valley.

And then the young male human was running towards him. *A boy with flaming red hair and piercing grey eyes. A boy with no fear – and a dagger in his hand.*

In that split second, thousands of years became merely the blinking of an eye. Karbel recognized the same fearless spirit of the boy. The same flash of blade that had ended his life centuries ago.

Fear gripped Karbel. In that instant, he feared what might be.

If he continued the attack, not only could his life

be ended once more, but far, far worse than losing his mortal life, this time, his eternal spirit-life could be ended too.

Could he risk that? Could he?

Karbel knew the answer.

Snarling and spitting, he backed off as the fearless young human came towards him, dagger raised.

Karbel could feel his strength beginning to drain. His mortality was diminishing again. The battle with the old warrior had taken much out of him. He had little strength to risk a fight with the young, fearless male. A fight he dare not lose.

His mortal body was beginning to ache – it was an effort to stay in this world.

Grant lunged, but the beast was swifter. It sprang, stretching its immense body as it leaped through the air, escaping the blade that Grant thrust at it.

Amanda gripped her broken branch in both hands, ready to swing it at the beast's head. But to her amazement, instead of coming at them, it began to back away.

Just a step backwards to begin with, and then another and another.

"Is...is it going?" Amanda barely dared to breathe.

Grant stood rigid, saying nothing, his arm and knife defiantly poised, still ready to strike.

The beast continued to back away, hissing and growling, but nevertheless backing away. And then, quite suddenly, it turned tail and bounded off through the trees.

For a second, Amanda and Grant were too shocked to move, and then they both gave chase, following the creature at a distance as it ran effortlessly through the woodland, agile, graceful, its shimmering form becoming fainter by the second.

It reached the edge of the forest and ran out into the evening light. By the time Amanda and Grant got to the clearing, the beast was bounding down the valley towards the loch.

Although its image was fading rapidly, they saw it wade into the shallows of the water, and scoop up and devour a fish.

It padded on towards the mountains, now little more than a pale flicker of light. But they could just make out its skilful leaps from rock to rock, climbing upwards, taking its zigzag path up the mountain, until it finally reached a ridge high, high above. And there it stood, looking down over the valley.

Away from human reach and mortal sight, Karbel looked down at the two humans standing beside the forest. Once again, humans had defeated him – humans with their weapons and their fearlessness.

In anger, he threw back his great head and howled out his rage and frustration, sending a startled hawk spiralling upwards on a warm current of air, alarmed by the disturbing presence in the breeze.

Then slowly, as the last rays of sunlight sparkled across the loch, Karbel gazed again over his domain. The blazing sunlight no longer caused him to blink or squint, it no longer dazzled and blinded. Gradually, his mortal troubles slipped away and the peace and contentment of the spirit world brought him comfort.

In this world he was safe. In this world he could see great distances, travel as fast as the wind, visible only as a fleeting shadow that might catch someone's eye and make them puzzle for a moment as to what they'd seen – or thought they'd seen.

The humans would venture no nearer. And here he would stay, enjoying his spirit world, his valley, for all eternity – or until he felt the urge to satisfy his hunting instincts once more.

But for now he settled down, safe in the knowledge that he, Karbel, would remain, long after all mortal humans were wiped clean off the Earth.

Chapter Thirteen

Amanda and Grant searched every inch of grass where the fight between Rab Stewart and the beast had taken place. But there was no sign of the old Scotsman or his sword, just a patch of crushed grass where the battle had raged.

"What if he's crawled off injured?" Amanda said as darkness began to fall and they still hadn't found him.

"There isn't a drop of blood. I don't understand it," Grant said, still searching. "We both saw him fall, so where did he go?"

"We'll have to tell Mum and Dad," said Amanda. "Even if they think we've both gone crazy, they'll have to help us look for him. They'll have to send for a search party or something."

Still stunned from all that had happened, they made their way back to the caravan. Their mum was just serving up the dinner.

She smiled. "Ah, right on time. Mr. Stewart said you'd be here in a minute."

Amanda and Grant stared at each other.

"Rab Stewart? He was here?" Grant exclaimed.

"Yes, just a minute ago. I think he was making peace with your dad. Said he wanted to apologize if he'd scared us with his stories the other day. He said you'd be here in a moment – and here you are. Wash your hands now before you eat."

Dad came strolling over, smiling. "He's not such a bad old stick. Bit of a character really."

"You definitely saw him?" Amanda questioned. "He was here, a minute ago?"

"Yes, I just said that," Mum laughed.

"And he was all right?"

"Very chirpy. I asked if he wanted to stay for dinner, but he said he wasn't hungry and that it was time he got home. Look, there he is now."

Amanda and Grant spun round.

To their astonishment, the old Scotsman was striding off towards the forest, stick swinging as if he were marching to some invisible band. He looked none the worse for his encounter with the beast.

As if sensing he was being observed, Mr. Stewart stopped and turned. There was a smile on his craggy old face. Looking directly at Amanda and Grant, he raised his hand and waved.

Automatically, they waved back.

And then he was gone.

"Do you think we'll see Rab Stewart again, Manda?" Grant asked, as they lay in their sleeping bags that night.

Amanda could see the stars through one of the rips in the side of the tent. Their parents hadn't seen the state of their tent yet. Amanda and Grant decided they would tell them everything – tomorrow. Although they probably wouldn't believe a word.

"No, I don't think we will see him again," Amanda replied, feeling relaxed now. No more fears and anxieties, they all seem to have faded away, just as the beast had faded away before their eyes.

"Was he real, Mand?"

She couldn't answer, and lay staring at a star through a slit in the tent before murmuring, "Real enough."

"Y'know something Mand…when I thought I'd actually have to fight the beast, I had this really strange feeling of *déjà vu*. Like I'd experienced it all before, only a long, long time ago."

"Maybe you have," she murmured.

He was silent for some minutes. Then softly he asked, "Do you think the beast will come back?"

"No, he won't come back," Amanda answered confidently. "At least, not in our lifetime."

"How can you be so sure?"

She smiled to herself. "I'm weird like that."

Grant chuckled softly. "Good job too. Goodnight, sleep tight."

"Hope the bugs don't bite," she finished the rhyme their parents used to say when they were small, while in her head, a tiny voice said, *Hope the beasts don't bite*.

USBORNE THRILLERS

MORE CHILLING STORIES TO KEEP YOU AWAKE AT NIGHT

MALCOLM ROSE

THE TORTURED WOOD

Who will be the next victim?

When Dillon's family moves into the tight-knit community of Bleakhill Top, Dillon soon discovers that the town is hiding a dark secret. His only refuge from the school bullies is in the wood that seems to be at the very heart of the mystery. There Dillon finds some startling, eerie carvings in the rotting stumps and fallen trees. When he starts to investigate the mysterious sculptor, he finds himself in mortal danger.

The chilling atmosphere and tense, dramatic storyline of *The Tortured Wood* grab you by the throat on the first page and don't let go until the last.

Publication July 2004

ISBN 0 7460 6035 1   £4.99

SANDRA GLOVER

Demon's Rock

There's something evil out there...

Bug and Mona have always known the stories about
Demon's Rock, and dismissed them as silly local
superstitions. But then a strange boy turns up on their
doorstep one night, completely confused and incoherent.
When Bug and Mona decide to investigate his story, they
are drawn to the rock, and discover that there is
something extraordinary going on out there...and it's
much, much scarier than anything the locals could have
dreamed up.

A dark and compelling novel that poses some thought-
provoking questions.

Publication August 2004

ISBN 0 7460 6037 8   £4.99

PAUL STEWART

the Curse of Magoria

Will anyone escape the deadly dance of time?

The local legend of Oberdorf tells the story of Magoria the Mathemagician who was once a powerful sorcerer intent on controlling time itself. But his experiments went disastrously wrong, and he unlocked a dangerous curse that could strike the remote community of Oberdorf at any time.

When Ryan arrives at the mountain village he has a terrifying nightmare in which he is trapped and hunted. Soon this nightmare becomes a reality and he realizes his visit might have deadly consequences…that he might have unleashed the Curse of Magoria.

A breathtaking tale of dark magic, adventure and revenge from the co-author of the hugely successful series *The Edge Chronicles*.

Publication August 2004

ISBN 0 7460 6232 X   £4.99

TERRY DEARY

The Boy Who Haunted Himself

There's no escape from the ghost in his mind

When Peter Stone arrives at Doctor Black's surgery after
responding to an advert promising to harness the power
of the mind, the squalid appearance and strange doctor
surprise him. But Peter really wants to change his life, so
he volunteers himself for a scientific experiment. And
things do change, but not in the way he hoped. Trapped in
an experiment that goes horribly wrong, Peter becomes
possessed by a spirit from the past, and must fight to
regain control of his own body and mind.

A truly creepy ghost story with a difference, from the
author of the spectacularly successful *Horrible Histories*.

Publication October 2004

ISBN 0 7460 6036 X   £4.99